I0571025

Baby Club

by

Mark Miller

Published and printed in the United States of America

Mark Miller

Baby Club

Published December 2009

ISBN: 978-0692006856

Dedicated to the child victims of abuse, neglect and abandonment.

Mark Miller

Baby Club

I know I look like hell, Lauryn said to herself as she tugged at a tight miniskirt, ran a hand through half wet, stringy, blond hair and pounded on Tynise's door.

Attractive, but not striking, she had always felt the need to enhance her best features with high heels and short skirts that showed off her legs. All of her clothes clung tightly to a five foot four inch frame that she just knew would look great in a bikini, if she ever got a chance to go to the beach.

The heavy, steel door shook and rattled loud enough to wake the dead, but she had to compete with the squeaky wheels of the L train, the screeching rug rats next door, and the yelling of a neighbor as he threatened his way into his own apartment. Lauryn pounded even harder when she remembered you could sleep through almost anything behind the thick concrete walls that made up the twenty story building. "Tynise," Lauryn called out, slapping the door.

"Ease up girl, dag." Tynise finally came to the door. "What you in such a hurry for anyway? I know you ain't itchin' to get to school, even if it is the first day."

"For real, I ain't in no hurry to sit in no boring classes," Lauryn replied. "At least it ain't gonna be our first year."

"I know, remember how scared we was comin' up from junior high. Everybody said Lincoln was rough as hell."

5

"Yeah, but we wasn't no punks about it. We tenth graders this year. We gonna be runnin' that school."

"I don't know about all that."

"I'm just playin'," Lauryn smiled. "I just wanna get at Dre and them. You know that boy is fine. I got my sights on all them ballers. I got me a list and Dre is at the top."

"A list."

"That's right. A list of ballers. Brotha gotta have somethin' goin' on, so he can buy me stuff."

"So, he gotta have money to get with you?"

"He gotta have somethin' goin' on, you know, basketball or hustlin' or whatever, it don't matter as long as he makin' that paper, you know what I'm sayin'. I'm tryin' to get with one that got a chance at the pros. Baby, I'll be straight."

"Please, ain't none of them fools goin' to the pros."

"Some of them got skills. You now Dre can straight up ball. I hear the scouts is checkin' him out already."

"Yeah, maybe, but you better have a plan B if you think you gonna be some kind of NBA trophy wife."

"He ain't gotta be no ball player, but he gotta be ballin', you know, and he gotta be a brotha. Kissin' a white boy is like eatin' a cracker without the salt, no flavor." Lauryn made a sour face.

"What you know about kissin' a white boy?"

"My little brother's friend had this fine older brother, anyway, we went out."

"And he was white?" Tynise turned up her nose.

"Yeah."

"That's a trip. I never seen you with a white boy. You know, there ain't too many of you around here. What's it like dating one?"

"Like I said, it's like cereal without the milk, like crackers with no cheese, like Kool-Aid without the sugar."

"Alright, already."

"You know what I'm sayin'."

"I wouldn't know. Why you dissin' your people like that, anyway? You white folks gotta stick together."

"I may be white, but I came up just like you and all the other brothers and sisters around here. It's my hood, too. I'm just tellin' it like it is. A white boy can't do nothin' for me."

"I feel you." Tynise raised her hand for a high five.

"Awe, man, why don't you go somewhere with all that," Lauryn snapped at a raggedy man relieving himself on a wall in front of the building. He was one of the many bums they would pass on their six block walk from their projects to Lincoln High School. The stench of his business floated through the air.

"Man, you stink," Tynise said and both giggled at the pitiful sight, their compassion hardened by years of exposure to scenes that should only be seen on TV.

Tynise and Lauryn were raised in the Harvey Projects with the stink of piss and stale alcohol saturating the walls and baseboards. They gad grown accustomed to the stench, like a farmer grows immune to the smell of the manure in his fields. They only noticed the odor when they were down wind of one of these bums.

"I guess it'll be okay gettin' back to school," Lauryn said.

"I know. We didn't do nothin' this summer but sit around. I wish I had some money to go away." Tynise looked up at the sky.

"Where would you go?"

"I don't know. I never been no place. Any place would be good. I don't care where. I really don't."

"I wanna go to the Greek Islands," Lauryn grinned.

"Yeah, why?"

"I saw that junk on *Wild On*. It was off the chain. They was takin' shots of this junk called *ozoo,* or whatever, and they was gettin' all tore up. All them ballers with they shirts off, hotty bodies."

"Is that all you think about?"

"What, like you don't like it."

"Not as much as you. You're like a sex fiend or somethin'."

"What, just cause I ain't 'fraid to get mine, I'm a fiend? I ain't fiendin'. I just know what I want."

"Yeah, I know, all the ballers."

The streets were full of kids dragging their feet to school, swarming like a stream of ants returning to the colony. They shouted out to each other and caught up on weeks past. They knew each other from around the neighborhood. The same faces going to the same places.

"We're supposed to meet Mari and Ruby out front, right?" Lauryn asked as they approached the school.

"That's what Mari said." Tynise looked at her watch. "Her bus should be here soon."

"It must be nice havin' a house of your own. She's very lucky."

"Yeah, but she's gotta share it with her sister, two brothers, both parents, her grandmother, and she said her cousin is stayin' with them now, too. That's eight people in that little, bitty house. You know they drive each other crazy."

"What you talkin' about?" Lauryn replied. "I know you don't have a lot of extra room at your place with your brother, sister and mother. It's gotta be better than livin' in them rat traps where we stay. A least she don't have to deal with them bums, addicts, freaks, hustlers, bangers, fools runnin' up and down the halls all day and night."

"Yeah, but she got all them gang bangers and drive bys on the south side."

"So do we."

"I know. I guess we do live in a rat trap." Tynise laughed.

"Hey, you just made a new name for the projects, *The Rat Trap.*"

"Now, Ruby, that girl's got it made."

"For real, she got that monster crib all to herself and it's in The Heights. Don't get me wrong, I love my girl, but why the hell she wanna come to school down here when she stay up there, livin' phat?"

"You know Ruby don't like to hang with all them white people out there, no offense."

"Please, you ain't offendin' me. I don't blame her, but she be takin' it to the extreme, you know, from the mansion to the hood, baby. I know they got some schools up there that ain't all white."

8

"I guess she's just tryin' to keep it real. It must be hard to feel black when you the only one around. What about you? If you was born in one of them rich neighborhoods, would you still hang out down here?"

"What you mean? You know my peoples is down here. I was born here. I don't know nothin' else."

"Yeah, but what if you was born in an all white neighborhood, with a bunch of other blond hair, blue eyed, little girls looking just like you. I bet you would've been a girl scout or somethin', runnin' around sayin', "Oh my God," and listenin' to, like, Lady Gaga, perfect little Barbie doll."

"Don't be tryin' me. I ain't no Barbie doll."

"Quit trippin'. I'm just playin'." Tynise detected Lauryn starting to swell. "There goes Ruby."

A smooth, black Mercedes pulled up to the curb and a tall, slender girl stepped out. Her eyes beamed when she saw Tynise and Lauryn. She slammed the car door without saying goodbye to the driver and ran over to her friends where they fell into each others arms in a group hug.

"Is that your car?" Lauryn asked, her eyes bugging out of her head. "That's a sweet ride."

"That's my mother's car," Ruby answered.

"You mean she actually brought you down here. Where's Anna?" Tynise said.

"For real, she ain't scared her ride gonna get jacked?" Lauryn warned.

"Hell yeah," Ruby smiled. "Look at her speed away. She's scared to death to come down here. That's why Anna usually drops me off, but she had the day off. I can't wait 'til I get my own car next year, when I turn sixteen," Ruby leered at the car as it drove away.

"They gonna buy you a car?" Lauryn asked.

"Yeah, probably an older BMW or whatever."

"A BMW, man, that's crazy. You got your mom all wrapped up," Lauryn said.

"I wish my mom would buy me a new pair of jeans," Tynise

9

joked."

"Yeah, well, they've always been good at throwing money around," Ruby looked at the ground.

"Is your father still in Iraq?" Tynise asked.

"Of course, where else would he be?" Ruby grumbled.

"At least you know where yours is," Lauryn shouted through the phony smile she wore whenever the subject came up.

"True that," Tynise gave Lauryn a pound, a show of unity between project sisters.

Hey, ain't that Mari? Mari, over here," Tynise called out.

Marisol rushed over as soon as her eyes caught Tynise's waving arms. Another group hug.

"What's wrong, Mari?" Tynise missed the bubbly, sparkle she was accustomed to seeing in Marisol's eyes.

"I don't know. It's just sad. I can't stop thinking about the baby." She clutched a wrinkled newspaper article in her hands.

"What's that?" Ruby gently opened Marisol's hand and read. "*Baby Found in Dumpster*. What kind of twisted freak would do that?"

"It ain't no twisted freak," Lauryn interrupted. "Remember that girl on *Oprah* that had her baby at prom and left it in the bathroom at school. Like they wasn't gonna know it was hers. Stupid."

"I remember that girl. She was probably freaked out about being a mother so young," Ruby said. "She was, like, our age."

"That don't matter," Marisol cried out. "She was the mama."

"Relax, Mari, dag," Lauryn patted her on the back. "It ain't like they was your babies."

"I'm gonna have a whole lot of babies with Hector." The corners of Marisol's lips curled into a slight grin.

"You mean someday, right?" Tynise asked.

"I don't know. I love Hector. I wanna marry him, like I can see it in my head and everything. We gonna have the wedding in my back yard. It's gonna be small back there, but it's not gonna be that many people. You guys gonna be my bride maids. I know the perfect color for the dresses, too. They gonna be pink and red. You know, very beautiful. I wanna have a lot of babies with Hector, four or five, maybe more."

"Damn, Mari, you trippin'. How you gonna marry the only guy you ever been with? You gonna make your first your last?" Lauryn asked.

"Why not? My mother got married at fifteen."

"Yeah, but that was in Mexico, wasn't it? It's common for women to get married young down there, especially back in the day," Ruby said.

"So, what does it matter if I fall in love in Mexico or here? You don't make no sense," Marisol snapped at them.

"It just seems like you'd be missin' out on a lot," Tynise said.

"Like what?" Marisol stood her ground, her eyes scanning the crowd.

"Relax, Mari," Tynise teased. "Hector would never be late. He's such a good little boy."

"Like all the fine brothas you ain't gonna be gettin' with," Lauryn answered. "Man, they got some dimes around here, fine in the face with a cute behind."

"Shut up, you stupid." Ruby gave her a high five. "You ain't lyin', but you still stupid. Oh, look at that one over there. I don't remember him from anywhere. There's just something about the tall ones."

"Where?" Tynise and Lauryn shamelessly stretched their necks.

"Over there," Ruby pointed, "the tall one with the shaved head. You can't miss him."

"Right, right, I see him," Lauryn smirked. "I bet he's gonna be on the team."

"Whatever. I'm gonna find Hector. I see you later." Marisol broke away to search through the mass of students.

"Man, that girl is sprung," Lauryn shook her head.

"Oooh, I know that's not Mike and them hittin' that forty this early in the morning." Tynise spotted a group of boys huddling in the corner. "See, I told you that boy wasn't about nothin'."

"What, just 'cause he likes to get his head back a little don't

11

mean he ain't about nothin'. That boy is fine," Lauryn replied.

"My mama said anyone who gets to sippin' before 5p.m. is beggin' for trouble," Tynise persisted.

"Come on, Lauryn. It's not even eight o'clock yet," Ruby agreed. "That's pretty bad."

"I don't think so. As a matter of fact." Lauryn pulled a small blunt out of her purse. "I don't see how anyone can sit through class with a straight head."

"You're not going to light that," Ruby warned.

"Why not?"

"Lauryn, put that thing away," Tynise commanded.

"Relax, grandma. It ain't like I'm the only one."

"She's right. I can smell it." Ruby sniffed the air.

"What, you think we was gonna get caught? Ain't nobody care around here." Lauryn took a long drag and held it out for Tynise and Ruby.

"It's way too early for me," Tynise shook her head. "It's too early for you, too."

"Please, it never too early to get your head straight." Lauryn took a long drag.

"I don't know why half these fools come to school. They just gonna mess up class, all high and everything, acting stupid. You see them boys over there. They ain't gonna do nothin' but sit in that corner and play craps all day," Tynise laughed as her tone relaxed. "I love to watch the school cops chase 'em up and down the halls."

Lauryn joined in on the laughter and looked to Ruby. "And you want to go to school down here. Baby, you gotta be crazy."

Chapter 2

Ruby hummed a soft melody, as she liked to do in the morning, when the house was quiet, except for the sounds of Anna making breakfast. Smooth, clear skin and a golden brown complexion that never needed make up, a gift from her mother's Asian heritage, meant it didn't take her long to get ready for school. That and her long, thick, perfectly straight hair were the only things Ruby had ever thanked her mother for.

Humming took the worry of today's cheer leading contest off her mind. It would be the fifth contest she had entered since starting to cheer two years ago. It would be the fifth contest her father missed. He had missed all her piano recitals when she was ten and dance programs when she was thirteen. He had missed the birthday parties, the honor roll report cards, and the first date. The humming helped her forget how much he had missed.

I don't care if he ever comes, she thought, then wondered why she ever wanted to see him. Nothing was ever good enough for the lieutenant colonel. She rummaged through her mental archives for a memory of a warm embrace, a pat on the back, a congratulations for doing it just right, but only retrieved his penetrating voice, hounding her to "do it right" or "do it again".

She had tried to harden her sensibilities to the constant criticism, to try harder and live up to his expectations, but it soon became easier to simply find an escape. An adventure on the wrong side of the tracks offered the perfect opportunity.

She told her mother she was going to the library to study and took the bus to a Martin Luther King Day celebration in a part of town her parents would never allow her to go. Her curiosity peeked at first, like a travel channel reporter tracking an undiscovered tribe. But the more time she spent "in the hood", the more it felt right. Like the natural way of things. Surrounded by people that looked like her, she was no longer an ink spot in a sea of white faces. It was new, dangerous, exciting and comfortable.

She felt the embrace of her race from her first basketball game at Lincoln High. She was at home sitting in the stands, like part of a giant blanket in a flowing wave of black and brown. Even the cheerleaders were Black or Mexican. The white faces where the spots, a sprinkling of tiny marshmallows in a huge pot of hot chocolate.

Budding hormones drew her to the playground, where the boys on the block played basketball. The bold, muscular, rough, slick talking boys noticed her immediately. They were nothing like the shy little boys in her all white neighborhood. She was intimidated at first, but Ruby was harder inside than she looked on the outside. She was the lieutenant colonel's daughter. Her quick wit and a take no mess attitude kept the wolves at bay.

The boys invited her to neighborhood parties. Ruby couldn't resist the attention or the hardness of their slender frames, but they were too aggressive, too blatant about the thoughts in their one track minds. Her body begged her to go with one of them into the smoke filled back rooms, just once, just to see what it was like. But, she knew better than to be labeled the neighborhood trick. She was still too afraid, not accustomed to their slang or the other girls' jealous glares. They drank big forty ounce bottles of cheap beer and smoked marijuana like they were on the set of a rap video. They were different in so many ways, but at her core, in the place were she felt most at ease, they were the same.

Her mother didn't notice the sneaking around or how much

school she was skipping until she began failing classes. Ruby was ready for the inevitable confrontation. She had a new attitude, fueled by the playground's gritty spirit. Mother shouted, Ruby shouted back.

Ruby detected the toll the shouting matches were taking and made her mother a deal. She would go back to school, but only if she could attend Lincoln. Mother was appalled by the idea. How would she face her country club friends? But she figured it was better than watching Ruby flunk out of school. She had no choice. Ruby didn't listen to her anymore and the lieutenant colonel wasn't there to enforce the rules.

"Ruby, be a dear and make sure Tabitha has enough food in her bowl tonight. I won't be home until late and you know how forgetful Anna can be sometimes." Ruby's mother tapped lightly on the door, but didn't wait for a response before entering her room.

"What do you mean? You're not coming to my cheer contest?"

"Contest?"

"My cheerleading contest after school, you know, the one I've been practicing so hard for."

"Of course, sweetie. I didn't forget. What time does it start?"

"Five o'clock."

"Oh, no, I have a fundraising dinner at the club tonight. I thought your thing would be right after school. I have to be at the club no later than five. I can't be late. I'm the chair on this one. My friends at the club will talk about me forever if anything goes wrong."

"God, who cares what those hags think," Ruby mumbled.

"Besides, I hate being down there after dark. It's depressing with all those bums and crazy looking people. It's not safe. Maybe if you went to a normal school instead of that school in the ghetto I would go to more of your things. Now you want me to go down to that place after dark. What time do I have to pick you up?"

"Forget it. I'll get a ride if it's gonna be so much trouble for you to break away from you country club hags."

"I don't know why you have to hang out with those people anyway. You know most of them are on drugs. I don't know why we agreed to let you go to school with all those criminals and gang people. They're down there shooting and killing each other and you want to be down there with them. You know those people have nothing to live for and they don't care if they take you with them. We didn't work all these years to give you the best of everything so you could waste your time associating with those people."

"What do you mean those people? Don't you mean Black people? Did you forget those people are my people? Or maybe you forgot you married a Black man."

"I didn't forget. I'm not prejudice. It has nothing to do with skin color. Those people are just lazy. They just sit around on the street corners all day drinking and smoking stuff. I see them. They have nothing on their minds."

"It's not that easy for them. You should see how they struggle and all the mess they have to put up with everyday. You wouldn't believe the way some of my friends live. You just pass by with your windows rolled up, but my friends have to live with all the bums and gang bangers, everyday. They didn't ask to be born down there, you know. How can you say they're all lazy? You don't know them. You never even bother to get out of your car. You don't know what's going on down there."

"I know they can't see an opportunity when it's staring them right in the face. We had nothing when my family came here from the Philippines. I worked hard growing up, slaving away in sewing factories for almost nothing. We were poor, but my mother and father showed me the opportunity here. I went to school and got a good job. Now look at us. We have a beautiful house and great friends, the American dream. If a little girl from the Philippines could see the opportunity, why can't those people hanging out on the street corners every day see it?"

"Well, Mom, not everyone is lucky enough to marry a lieutenant colonel with a big, phat crib in The Heights. You definitely do know how to take advantage of an opportunity."

"That's not fair. I worked very hard as a nurse before I met your father. I knew letting you go to school down there was a big mistake.

16

It was your father's decision. He said it was the only way to get you to stay in school, but I've always been against it."

"At least I can be myself there. People down there don't know how to be phony."

"Look, honey, I know you feel out of place here sometimes and I know how important it is for you to have Black friends, but there are a lot of other ways to reconnect with the Black community without having to go to school with drug dealers and gang people. You're only fifteen years old. I can't believe he agreed to this non sense."

"Well, he did."

"Sure he did. He's not the one who's going to have to claim you at the hospital when one of those gang boys tries to kill you. No, he'll be thousands of miles away. At least he won't be able to blame it on me. It's not safe down there. I told him. Look, honey, I've got to go. How are you getting home from your thing?"

"Marisol's mother will bring me."

"Fine, honey, I've got to go. Please be careful, okay." She rushed out the door leaving Ruby alone with the realization that she had the night free.

Chapter 3

An anxious tension filled the air whenever the gym held a full crowd. Everybody remembered Tanya, the innocent ten year old who caught the bullet intended for a rival gang member at the homecoming game last year. Nobody talked about it much anymore, but every now and then someone slammed a door or made a loud thump, mimicking the all too familiar sound that sunk the crowd into a nervous hush.

Ruby methodically practiced her steps and did some last minute stretching on her own. It kept her mind focused and her eyes off the crowd she might be tempted to scan for the mother and father she knew were not there.

"What you doing over here by yourself?" Marisol came up behind her.

Marisol was the first girl Ruby met when she joined the team. The two had grown to think of each other as sisters.

"I see your family's all here." Ruby couldn't help but feel a little jealous when she saw Marisol's sister, brothers, cousin, both parents, and Hector in the crowd, smiling and waving. "They must really support you."

"They come to all my things. Is your mother gonna come?"

"No, she said she had country club business to attend to."

"I'm sorry, Ruby. I know you want her to come."

"Whatever."

"There you are. We've been looking for you," Tynise said as she and Lauryn ran up on them. "You guys ready to win this thing."

"I guess," Ruby answered.

"It's no guessing. We gonna win," Marisol replied cheerfully. "Come on, Ruby, you know we gonna win."

"Does it really matter? I mean, really," Ruby moaned.

"I'm with Ruby," Lauryn jumped in. "Antonio's party gonna be off the chain tonight."

"For real, that boy knows how to throw down." Tynise agreed.

"So, what's the plan?" Ruby asked.

"Hector said he gonna drive us," Marisol said.

"Cool, as long as he don't bring that buck toothed, midget boy with him." Lauryn cringed. "He's always tryin' to get with me, with his broke self."

"Hey, leave Ricardo alone. That's Hector's primo," Marisol shouted over their laughter.

"I don't care what he is. That boy can't do nothin' for me," Lauryn persisted. "He's always starin' at me and tellin' me how pretty I am and junk like that."

"So, what's wrong with that?" Marisol asked. "Ricardo is a nice guy. He just don't know how to talk to girls, that's all. The only reason he tell you all that nice stuff is 'cause he like you. He just don't know how to say it."

"Tell me about it," Lauryn laughed. "That boy ain't got no game."

"See, that's your problem," Tynise jumped in. "You don't know what to do when a nice guy wants to get with you. I bet that boy would treat you like a queen. He would worship the ground you walk on."

"Please, I would walk all over that fool. I bet he'd be callin' me all the time, tellin' me how much he loves me and junk like that. I hate that mess."

"That's all wrong, Lauryn," Ruby cut in. "You have this great guy, willing to do anything for you, and you don't want anything to do with him? You could at least use him up a little before you toss him to the side."

"You feel me." Lauryn smiled at Ruby. "I just wanna a little challenge, that's all. I don't want no boy droolin' all over me."

"And that's why you keep gettin' burned," Tynise said. "You keep chasin' all them sweet talkin' players, then you wonder why you get played."

"Yeah, but this time I'm gonna be doin' the playin'," Lauryn replied defensively.

"That don't make no sense," Marisol said. "That's why I go for Hector. He's so good to me. He don't mess around with no other girls. He just go to school, go to football, go to his job, then he come to see me. He don't have no time for no other girl."

"I'm so happy for you," Lauryn sneered sarcastically. "You think you got it made, but you better watch that boy. Hector might be a nice guy and all, but he's still a guy and all guys cheat. It's in their blood. They can't help it. And you the only one Hector's been with. What you gonna do when he starts thinkin' about doin' it with other girls?"

"He's not gonna do that. That's not Hector."

"No, you wait and see. You think you gonna be the only girl he ever does it with in his whole life. Come on now. I know you ain't that stupid," Lauryn jabbed with a smug look on her face.

"You better shut up," Marisol snapped. "You don't know Hector. You just jealsous."

"Okay, that's enough. Dag, Lauryn, what's wrong with you?" Tynise stepped in.

"Come on, Mari, we have to warm up. We'll be on in a few minutes." Ruby tugged at Marisol's arm and they walked away.

"Why you gotta be so mean, Lauryn?" Tynise asked. "You know that wasn't right."

"I'm sick of her goin' on about her Hector. It's enough already."

"You can't be mad at her just 'cause she's in love. Can't you see how happy Hector makes her? Let her have her happiness."

"Whatever. I ain't sweatin' that girl." Lauryn turned her head and began scanning the crowd.

The gym was filled with mothers, fathers and younger brothers and sisters. *They ain't no cute guys her.* Lauryn thought and closed her eyes. She pretended the rumbling of the crowd was the crowd at the party, jamming to a D.J. on a packed dance floor. She ran through her hit list of ballers, all the guys she hoped were going to be at the party, and tried to remember which ones had girlfriends. She slowly opened her eyes and leered at the cheerleaders. *They ain't about nothin'. Why the ball players always go for them first? Like milk and cookies.*

The competition was tough, but neither Ruby nor Marisol expected to win. Central High had won two years in a row. Their coach was an Olympic gymnast many, many years ago. She never won a gold medal, but she had taught them some incredible flip routines.

"You guys did great," Tynise said as she and Lauryn jumped off the bleachers on to the hard wood court.

"Yeah, right," Marisol laughed. "You didn't see me slip? I almost fall down in front of everybody."

"Oh, well, better luck next time," Ruby said. "Where's Hector? I'm ready to get outta here."

"Me too," Lauryn agreed. "What time is it?"

"It's only eight. The party won't be jumpin' off 'til a least ten," Tynise answered as if she could read Laruyn's mind.

"That's cool. I can get my party on tonight," Ruby said. "My mom will be at the country club all night. She said they're having a fundraising meeting, but those meetings only take about an hour. Then they sit up there all night playing cards and getting drunk as a skunk."

"My mom won't be home from work until at least one or two." Tynise shook her head. "They be workin' her like a slave down at the diner."

"You know my moms don't care," Lauryn said. "She might not even come home tonight. What about you, Mari? Your parents keep you on a pretty tight leash."

21

"I just tell them I'm spending the night at Ruby's. They like me to go up there. They say it's good for me to get a taste of the good life."

"It's on then," Lauryn shouted. "Let's go find Hector."

They cruised around in Hector's pea green 1982 Oldsmobile Cutlass Supreme for a couple of hours before they got to the party. There was no particular destination in mind. Hector, Marisol, and Ricardo sat in the front seat with Tynise, Ruby, and Laruyn in the back. The car rocked like a boat when Hector took a curb too fast, but it really took off when he stomped on the gas. Hector called it his great all American, old school, muscle car, but the girls just knew it as the perfect party ride.

"Slow down, Hector," Ricardo pleaded as the car drove by a group of pretty girls standing outside the corner store. He had already been rejected by Lauryn, Tynise and Ruby multiple times, so he knew better then to hit on them. "Man, I ain't gonna get no play ridin' in this old rust bucket."

"It ain't the car, fool," Hector laughed at him. "Don't blame my ride 'cause your rap is weak."

"What you talkin' about, fool. My junk is tight," Ricardo stuck his head out the window. "Hey, what you up to tonight, beautiful?"

"You need to go somewhere with that, 'what you up to beautiful'," Lauryn teased. "Them girls got names and I bet ain't none of them answer to hey beautiful."

"That's right, Ricardo," Ruby said. "You have to treat them with respect. Then they might consider talking to you."

"Please, I know what the women like. My game is tight," Ricardo defended himself.

"Oh, yeah, you got 'em fallin' all over you," Tynise giggled.

"Leave him alone," Marisol said, joining in on the laughter as the car approached the party.

"Oh, yeah. That's what I'm talking about. Ain't that Jerome," Lauryn grinned as she checked out the scene.

"No way. That ain't him, is it?" Tynise squinted her eyes.

"That's him. Damn, that boy is fine," Ruby said. "When did he

22

get that ride?"

"He just got that Escalade. Man, that thing's tricked out. Look at them rims. They gotta be 24s and spinners, too. Man, that junk is tight," Hector said.

"Jerome must be comin' up in the game. I mean I knew he was gettin' big time, but, he's straight ballin', for real," Lauryn declared.

"See, man, that's what I need," Ricardo said. "If we was rollin' in that ride, I'd pull all the hotties. Man, I gotta get a ride like that, for real."

"Hey man, all you gotta do is move in on his turf and you too can live the American dream, providing the valuable service of selling rocks to the people," Hector joked.

"Shut up, man," Tynise barked at him. "That mess ain't even funny. I better not ever hear of any of you getting' caught up in that mess. You know what that junk can do to you. We've all seen it. That fool's getting' rich takin' from his own people. Don't even play like that, for real."

"I don't care how he makes that paper as long as he shares it with me," Lauryn smiled, her eyes fixated on Jerome. "The streets done took enough out of me. It's about time I get some back."

"That ain't even right," Tynise grunted.

"Hurry up and park the car, Hector," Lauryn ordered him. No time to waste. She had zoomed in on her target.

The party was at the house of one of Hector's teammates. As one of the captains on the football team, Hector commanded a certain respect. It was standing room only inside and the music was so loud they felt its vibration moving through their bodies. They worked their way through the smoky, dimly lit room, past the gyrating bodies that couldn't tell the difference between a hallway and a dance floor, and into the kitchen.

"Did you bring the wine, Hector," Marisol asked.

"Yeah, my brother hooked us up. Here you go."

He pulled out a bottle of Marisol's favorite, Boones Farms, and put the rest in the refrigerator. All the girls drank the same sweet, fruity wine. It came in a variety of flavors, but the favorite seemed to be Strawberry Hill. Hector and Ricardo drank bottles of Corona. No real man would ever be caught dead drinking a wine cooler when a perfectly good beer was around. Everybody was drinking or smoking something. Someone passed around a blunt. Hector and Marisol never touched the stuff, but passed it on down the line. Tynise and Ruby each took a small puff, but Lauryn took in a big drag and barely avoided coughing smoke all over everybody.

"Take it easy, girl," Hector laughed. "How high you need to get anyway?"

"Don't worry about me. I can handle my bizness," Lauryn said confidently. Her eyes trailed Jerome as he moved across the room.

Jerome grew up with all the boys on the team. He was the best athlete on their youth club football and basketball teams, but he was hooked to the fast bucks and excitement of selling drugs. He had no choice, coming from a family of gang bangers. It was in his blood.

"Where you goin'?" Tynise asked Lauryn as she walked away from the group.

Lauryn waved back without answering. She smiled as she approached Jerome with a one liner that had helped her break the ice in the past. "I like your kicks. Are they new?" she asked.

"You know I gotta keep it fresh, shorty," Jerome said as he and his friends checked Lauryn out.

The more they looked, the more she wanted them to look.

"I love your Escalade. It's the tightest ride I've ever seen. What's it like inside?" She batted her eyes, twirling her long hair between thin fingers.

"You wanna ride, shorty? You can see for yourself. Come on, let's roll," Jerome said.

He smirked at his friends and turned to walk toward his car. Lauryn followed behind him like a lap dog.

"Lauryn stepped up into the car. High from the blunt, her eyes grew large as saucers as the bright dashboard lights danced through her mind. Her body writhed in comfort as she sunk into the soft, caressing leather. Jerome looked at her and smiled.

They drove around the neighborhood drinking beer, smoking a

blunt and listening to the state of the art stereo system. Jerome got off on explaining all the gadgets and toys on the car. Lauryn latched on to every word, giggling and flipping her hair back to expose a well practiced smile. The munchies guided them to Burger King where they grubbed out on big, fat cheeseburgers, fries, and onion rings.

Lauryn didn't think when she was invited to the back seat of the car. She wanted him as much as he wanted her. When he finished, Jerome jumped back into the front seat and lit up the blunt he left in the ashtray.

They drove in silence back to the party, listening to the pulse banging through the speakers. A silly grin spread across Jerome's face. Lauryn sat, expressionless, looking through the window. She asked to be dropped off at home instead of going back to the party. She was pleasantly surprised when, just as she stepped out of the car, Jerome handed her a blunt and asked if she wanted to hang out sometime next week.

Lauryn grinned as she stared at the chipped concrete covering the twenty story building. It was early, but the night had been perfect. Jerome picked her over all the girls at the party. She had bagged her prize. She didn't want to go back to the party, but she didn't want to go inside.

Even though she had lived in the project most her life, she never felt safe there by herself on a Friday night. There was too much going on, the working girls in their tight shorts, high heels and fish net stockings, the wandering addicts shamelessly begging to do anything for any scrap of money, the drunken men roaming the streets, hollering at anything female.

She shared the sixteen floor ride to her apartment with some passed out drunk. The elevator crept upward at a snails pace and she closed her eyes to pass the dreaded time. She was back inside Jerome's Escalade, the leather surrounding her body once again, like a plush cocoon.

She didn't bother to turn on the light when she entered the apartment. The place always looked like hell and she'd rather not endure the sight of scampering cockroaches. The stench of a sink full of dirty dishes nobody had the motivation to clean filled the air, but she didn't care. It was a place to crash, alone, where she wouldn't be bothered.

Her mother wouldn't come home until early in the morning, after a long night of dancing at the strip club. Then she would sleep all day, usually with some guy lying next to her, but it was hardly ever the same guy.

Lauryn got undressed, fell into bed, and puffed on the blunt Jerome gave her. She hoped to forget about the paint peeling from the walls, the inevitable meeting with whatever half naked man emerged from her mother's bedroom, and the constant commotion of traffic in and out of the dealer's apartment next door. Her mind drifted to her thirteen year old brother, Billy, who had been locked up in juvi for six months for selling drugs and stealing cars. She remembered how tight they were, how tough he was and how he was always there for her when their mother was never around.

She puffed and imagined herself riding around in Jerome's big, shiny Escalade, like she was the queen of the hood and fell asleep in her own little fairy tale kingdom.

Chapter 4

Tynise had to be home by 5p.m. on school days to meet the bus that dropped off her eight year old sister and eleven year old brother from the after school program at church. She usually liked to hang out with Lauryn, Marisol or Ruby for a while, but recently she had been enjoying the solitude of an empty apartment. She lived on the eighth floor, but one floor was just the same as the other. Their family didn't have much of anything, but thanks to her mother's constant nagging, the apartment was always clean. Tynise didn't mind. The cleaning made living there almost bearable. Her mother always said, "Just 'cause we're poor as dirt, don't mean we have to live in it."

Tynise lingered in front of her full length mirror a little longer than usual. She could hear *Oprah, Monique,* and *Tyra* telling her to love herself and accept her body just the way it is. She accepted that she was twenty pounds heavier and four inches shorter than her best friends, but love it, never.

Them boys like what I got, she convinced herself as she ran her hands across a healthy chest and what she called her sister booty. *I ain't that big. They go for my goodies, but they don't want but one thing. I gotta look like Mari or Ruby to keep a boyfriend, perfect cheerleader bodies.*

I ain't goin' on no diet. I ain't givin' up my food just 'cause they can't see all this. She remembered all the boys who compared her back side to Jennifer Lopez and Beyonce. *Somebody gonna love me for what I got.*

Her solitude was abruptly interrupted by her brother and sister, Quincy and Jasmine, bursting through the door.

"I want a popsicle," Jasimne said throwing her book bag on the floor.

"You better pick that up. I just finished cleaning up this place," Tynise barked.

Quincy marched by without saying a word, put down his back pack and turned to head back out the door.

"Where you goin'?" Can't you speak to nobody? Hold up. Have you done your homework yet?" Tynise blocked him at the door.

"Yeah, man, I did it at the church. I'm gonna hang with my boys, alright," Quincy responded defiantly. "There ain't no place for me to hang here, is there?" He looked around the small two bedroom apartment. Mom's got a room. You and Jasmine got a room. Oh yeah, let me show you my room." Quincy walked over to the couch. "What, you think we gonna be hangin' out here."

"Who you hangin' out with?" Tynise demanded to know.

"Don't worry about it," he answered.

"I'm gonna worry about it, you're my brother."

"Jimmy and them."

"What you doin' with them?" You ain't sellin' are you? You better not be sellin'. Have you lost your mind? Mama's gonna tear you up when I tell her."

"What she gonna do? How she gonna stop me when she ain't never here? Man, I'm tired of not havin' nothin'. Jimmy's been showin' me how to get mine. You know you ain't gonna get nothin', if you don't take nothin'," Quincy exclaimed as he broke away from Tynise and stomped out the door.

"Is that what that fool's been teachin' you? Come back here," Tynise shouted out to him as he disappeared down the hallway.

Her heart broke as she thought of their older brother, Darnell, serving 15 to 25 on a manslaughter charge for killing a rival gang member. A rush of sadness flowed through her body when she thought of the void his absence left and realized Darnell would be at least thirty three years old before they even thought about letting him out. Darnell never listened to anyone, so much like Quincy is today.

Tynise slammed the door and stared out the window at the streets that had claimed a stake on her family.

Jasmine didn't seem to be phased by their little arguments. She had learned to lose herself in the TV. She loved B.E.T., especially the rap videos and any reality show she could find. Jerry Springer was her favorite.

A familiar knock on the front door interrupted Tynise's thoughts. She immediately knew it was Lauryn, her best friend since the second grade. Lauryn usually came by everyday. It was better than sitting alone in her dingy apartment.

Tynise opened the door to a glassy eyed Lauryn.

"Hey, what you up to?" Lauryn slurred.

"What's up?"

"You got to try this. Oh, baby, I'm swayin'."

"I can see that. You need to lay off that mess."

"You need to try this, here." Lauryn held out a blunt.

"Put that junk away. Don't you see Jasmine sittin' right over there."

"Oh, sorry. We'll save it for later."

Tynise, Jasimne and Lauryn sat silently on the couch watching Jerry Springer. They stared at the TV in a visual trance as they tried to figure out why the scrawny, hyper, little, white guy couldn't see how the loud, over weight, he/she stomping around on the stage wasn't a man.

"How the hell could he not know?" Tynise screamed at the TV.

"For real, look at that face. That's a man face if I ever saw one," Lauryn said.

"And her shoulders are all big and everythin'. Yep, that's a man," Jasmine joined in.

"You know they been kissin' and lovin' on each other and he gonna say he didn't know," Lauryn laughed. "You know that fool

29

knew. He just wanted to get his freak on."

"I know," Tynise laughed back. "He knew what he was gettin'. He's just playin' it off on TV, but I bet he's gonna stay with that man after the show."

"Don't you mean that woman?" Lauryn asked.

"No, I mean that man. That's a man right there. He's got a ding-a-ling, don't he? If he got a ding-a-ling, then he's a man. I don't care what you dress him up as."

"I hear you," Lauryn agreed. "Man, that's crazy. At least I know what I am. That poor thing don't know if he want to be a man or a woman or what."

"So confused," Tynise said as her tone suddenly changed. "At least someone's life is more messed up than mine."

"Please, you want to hear some craziness?" Lauryn asked.

"What?"

"Guess who I got with at the party."

"I wondered what happened to you. Who?"

Still high from the blunt she was smoking earlier, Lauryn started laughing so hard she could barely pronounce the name, "Jerome."

"Oooooh, I knew it." Tynise's ears perked up. "What you doin' with that dealer? You tryin' to end up in a drive by?"

"Don't get caught up in the game," Jasmine said, nonchalantly joining the conversation.

"What you know about the game?" Tynise asked.

"For real, you need to keep quiet when grown folks is talkin'," Lauryn snipped.

"I don't see no grown folks," Jasmine quipped and snapped her head around.

"Just mind your own business," Tynise sneered. "Come on, Lauryn. Let's go to my room. And I better not catch you at the door."

"Whatever." Jasmine frowned, but rebounded quickly. She had Jerry Springer to keep her company.

"Lock the door," Tynise instructed Lauryn as they rushed into her room. "Tell me what happened."

"He took me for a ride in that super fine Escalade. Baby, that thing is tricked out. I thought them leather seats was gonna swallow me up. Then he lit up this big, fat blunt and it was on."

"You laid down for him?" Tynise was disappointed, but not surprised.

"It don't mean nothin'." Lauryn's face turned cold, but only for a second then popped into a conniving grin. "You should've seen me ridin' in that Escalade though. I was the queen of the hood."

"How could you just go with him like that? You givin' it away for a ride in a nice car?"

"It ain't like that. It's more like I'm using him."

"What do you mean?"

"He could have any girl he wants cruisin' in that sweet ride and he picked me. Now everybody can see I roll with the best. I get instant respect being down with Jerome."

"He can't get any girl," Tyinse argued. "Don't you know he's gonna think you're a trick, givin' it up so fast."

"I couldn't help it. It's the challenge, you know what I mean. Jerome's got more juice than anyone else on the block. If I get with him, that'll make me the trick with the most juice. You know he asked me to hang out next week, so I must have somethin' goin' on."

"You got too much goin' on to be nobody's trick, Lauryn. That's my point. Why the hell you wanna hang out with the biggest dealer on the block? Don't you know how much mess you can get into?"

"Why not? I ain't got no where else to go. It ain't like I'm goin' to college like you or Ruby so what do I care."

Tynise bowed her head. She knew Lauryn was right. Lauryn had never been any good at school, even when she used to try.

"Not everybody is made to go to college, Lauryn. There's nothing wrong with that, but there's a lot more you can do other than going to college. All you have to do is learn how to use a computer, you know, Microsoft and all that. You could get a good job in an office or something. Remember what that lady said at career day."

"Yeah, right, like you could see me in some office. I'd go crazy."

"You could learn a trade like working on cars. Mechanics make good money."

31

"I ain't no good at that kind a stuff."

"You could be a nurse."

"I don't think so. My homeboy's friend said his sister took them tests and they was hard as hell."

"There's got to be something you can do. We'll figure it out."

"There is something. Tynise, I want a baby. I could be a good mother. I know I could. I wouldn't do like mine and stay out all night and be all stupid and drunk all the time. I'm gonna raise my baby right," Lauryn looked at Tynise, her eyes pleading for affirmation.

"Come on, Lauryn, you ain't ready for a baby. You gonna get a job?"

"Maybe, 'til then I'll just get on the system. I'll get a side hustle doin' hair or somethin'. Me and my baby gonna be straight."

"Yeah, but are you ready for all that responsibility?"

"I ain't got nothin' else to do. I already thought about it. Look, you got your moms, brother and sister. My bro is locked up and my moms ain't never around. I ain't goin' to college or nothin'. I ain't never gonna get outta the hood. Even if I do hair and stuff, 'cause I'm good at it, I gotta stay here 'cause this is where all my customers stay. No matter what I do I can't get outta the hood. It's like I'm a rat stuck in a big, crazy maze. No matter where I turn, I always hit a dead end."

"A maze, huh. I never thought about it like that, but I feel you. It's hard as hell to try to figure a way out of this place. College ain't gonna be easy. Sure I'm smart for around here, but I'm gonna be in there with all them really smart kids from good schools. You know they ain't teachin' us right at Lincoln. Those books are all old and tore up. I'm gonna look like a fool compared to them smart kids. Don't be surprised if I fail out and end up right back here with you."

"That's alright. We can do our own thing here. We'll open a hair shop. With your smarts, you could handle the bizness part of it and I could do all the hair. We could get paid, for real. We'll be the biggest rats in this maze."

Tynise nodded, a silent acknowledgment of her scattering college dreams. "You still got some of that blunt?" Tynise held out her hand. "You know you just came up with a new name for the projects."

"What's that?"

"We'll call it *The Maze.*"

Chapter 5

Hector and Marisol snuggled up on a small couch watching a comedy about a single man who adopted seven foster children.

"Man that's a lot of kids," Hector said as he stared at the TV.

"It's a great thing that man did. He take in those kids so all the brothers and sisters can stay together," Marisol said squeezing Hector around the waist. "I can see you doing something like that."

"No you can't"

"Yes I can. I bet you gonna make a great father. Don't you want kids?"

"Sure, I guess, doesn't everybody, but some day, not today. I have to finish college first. And not so many. Seven kids at one time, man, that's bananas."

"I want a whole lot of kids."

"How many you talkin' about?"

"I want at least five."

"Five, no way. You'd get too big and fat, like my Aunt Sophia. She looks like a bean bag or something."

"Oh, that's so mean. Don't talk about your tia like that."

"Tia's cool and all that, but you know she's big. She's so big you can't even pull her up on the internet. You gotta iron her pants in the driveway. When the kids see her coming, they yell, 'Hey Kool-Aid'."

"Aye, stop it, Hector. That's your tia. Don't be so mean," Marisol giggled along with Hector. "What if I got that fat? You gonna leave me?"

"In a minute," Hector said, still laughing. "I can't be seen with some big, fat chic."

"Damn, Hector. Why you gotta say it like that," Marisol snapped at him. "You know every woman gonna gain some weight when she have a baby. You can't help it. So if I give you a baby, you just gonna leave me?"

"No, baby, quit trippin'. I was just joking."

"Aye, stop it, you gonna break something." Marisol giggled at her six year old twin brothers.

The two were inseparable, running around, bouncing off the furniture, and slapping each other with anything they could pick up. Marisol's thirteen year old sister, Claudia, was also there with a couple of her friends from school.

There seemed to be constant bickering in the house ever since their ten year old cousin, Belinda, came to stay with them. Her parents fell to the lure of drugs so Marisol's father took her in before child protective services got involved. Belinda had not stopped following Claudia around since she came. Of course no burgeoning, self-reliant teenager wanted some ten year old kid following her around all the time. It had turned into the clash of the century. The house had always been noisy, but now it was like a crowded kindergarten before nap time.

"Man, these kids are buggin' out. Do they ever shut up?" Hector groaned.

"Leave them alone, they're just playing," Marisol smiled at her brothers wrestling on the floor. "I don't care about the noise. It makes the house alive."

"They don't get on your nerves?"

"No, es mi familia. I like it when the house is full. Hector, we been together for, like, two years. Don't you ever think about a family?"

"Yeah, someday, but there's plenty of time for that. I'm only

35

seventeen and you're only fifteen. Why are you even thinking about that right now? Awe, no, you're not trying to tell me something are you? Please say no."

"No, Hector. I'm just daydreaming. Every girl dreams about having a baby and a family someday."

"Do all girls want to have babies?"

"Si, silly, that's what makes you a woman."

"And you want five?"

"At least five."

"Now, see, that's crazy. Then our house would be like this house."

"That's right." A big smile crossed Marisol's face as she watched her brothers, sister and cousin all caught up in their little battles.

"Man, I bet those rug rats drive your parents crazy," Hector pointed to the twins. "I bet they have no time to themselves. They probably never get any privacy. I'm in no hurry to be one of those old married couples that don't even have the time to do it anymore."

"Oh, you guys act like you gonna explode if you don't get it. You can go without it. You waited six months before you got me."

"Eight months," Hector corrected her. "Baby, why did you make me wait so long? That makes me mad when I think about it."

"I was young, Hector. I wasn't ready. It was worth the wait, wasn't it? I mean, I made up for all that time."

Hector smiled. He couldn't help himself when he looked into Marisol's deep, brown eyes. "You really want five kids? Baby, I don't think you thought this one through too good. Do you really want to be chasing those little crumb snatchers around all day? And what about me? Did you ever think how much money I would have to make to raise five kids?"

"We'll get by. My parents don't make a lot of money and they have all of us."

"Yeah, but don't you want to get out of the hood one day. I know I do. That's what we need to be working on right now, you know. You have to keep your grades up so you can into a good college.

You know you're gonna need to get a scholarship. I'm gonna get one and you can get one, too. You just gotta know how to work the system. They got all kinds of stuff out there for us ghetto kids."

"Like scholarships and stuff."

"Yeah, my Pops is on all that stuff. He says there ain't no way he's paying all that money for school when they're putting all that cash on the table. I just have to keep my grades up. I'm getting out of here, baby, and you're coming with me. You're smart enough. You just have to keep your grades up, too."

"Mari, set the table for dinner. Your father will be home soon," a voice interrupted from the kitchen.

"Aye, Mama, why can't Claudia do it? It's her turn."

"Come on, Mari. She has her friends over. Don't give me a hard time. You should set a good example for your sister."

"Doing her work is setting a good example?" Marisol moped into the kitchen.

She stood next to her mother in front of an assortment of vegetables spread out on the kitchen counter. It was hard to tell them apart from behind with their long, black locks streaming half way down flawlessly curved backs. If you looked closely you may notice slight gray streaks hiding like pearls of wisdom in her mother's hair. She was a beautiful woman who had been able to preserve most of her girlish figure after having four kids. She was only sixteen when she had Marisol. Claudia came two years later. Her body seemed to be able to just mold back into place then, as if it were made out of elastic, but things changed after the twins. Marisol noticed the difference in pictures. Her mother sagged in places where she used to be upright and tight. To Marisol, her mother still looked amazing. After having four kids, her skin still looked as soft and smooth as her own. She figured if her mother could have four and still look so great, she could easily have five.

"You making menudo?" Marisol asked.

"Yes, you know it's your father's favorite."

"Papi." The twins rushed the door as soon as they heard it creak open. They clung to their father's waist like it had been ten years since they had seen him and they wouldn't see him for another ten years if they let him go.

Papi used to run the streets in his younger days. As an adult, he was resolved and content with his place in life. Most of the cholos he grew up with were either dead or in prison. He considered himself lucky to have survived. Fortunately, he discovered a natural talent for working with cars. He turned his hobby into a steady career as head mechanic at a large auto repair shop. He married the only girl on the block that ever really kept his fire burning and never looked back.

The family sat down at a large table they placed in a space off the kitchen. The house was modest, a small kitchen, a family room with a big, square 26 inch TV, a stereo system so old it still played vinyl records, two small couches, a faded, wooden coffee table, and a beer stained, plaid, cloth recliner that everyone knew was reserved for Papi. The table served as the meeting place for the family every day when Papi got home from work. Marisol and Claudia knew to be home by seven for dinner or they would answer to Papi.

Chapter 6

The girls usually hung out at each other's houses or at the local park after school. It wasn't a traditional park. There was no grass, no trees, no cool, fall breeze, no fresh water pond where you could feed the ducks or even a fountain where you could toss a penny and make a wish. The monkey bars, a metal slide and a small set of baby swings were the only clues that this actual was a park, but nothing about this space was safe for a baby or any other child. It was hard to take more than a few steps on the hard concrete without seeing a syringe or feeling the crunch of glass under your feet.

"That's what I'm talkin' about," Lauryn said as she fixed her eyes on a group of boys playing basketball, bickering over who fouled who.

"Don't you ever give it a rest," Tynise looked at Lauryn with a familiar expression of disappointment. "So, you gonna tell 'em about what you did at the party?"

"What did you do?" Marisol asked.

"Go ahead, tell them," Tynise challenged Lauryn.

"I got with Jerome, that's all."

"What do you mean you got with him?" Marisol asked.

"I think you know what she means," Ruby replied with the same disappointed expression Tynise wore on her face.

"You had sex with him?" Ruby exclaimed. "When? Where?"

"He took me for a ride in that fine Escalade. I don't know. It was somethin' about them soft, warm seats. You know, ridin' around in that shiny car like I was a movie star or somethin'."

"So, all it takes is a ride in a nice car?" Ruby replied angrily. "You know he's gonna think you're a slut."

"I think they already know," Marisol sighed.

"What do you mean by that," Lauryn asked.

"Please, you been givin' it away like food stamps since the sixth grade," Tynise jumped in. "Remember when Ms. Robinson caught you and that boy in the bathroom at school. What were you doin', playin' doctor?"

"Come on now," Lauryn defended herself. "We was just playin' around. We didn't know what we was doin'."

"You never gonna find a good boy if you keep giving it away like that," Marisol added. "I made Hector wait eight months before we did it. You can't just give it away. Then it don't mean nothing."

"It don't mean nothin' noway," Lauryn grumbled. I ain't gonna find nobody like Hector. At least if I can get in with Jerome, I get to shine in that fine ride."

"Tynise, is that you?" a deep voice crept into Tynise's ear.

Tynise didn't turn around at first, but she recognized the voice. The looks on Ruby's, Marisol's, and Lauryn's faces confirmed her suspicion. It was Tyree, Tynise's old boyfriend. They went out for four months last year, but to Tynise it felt like a lifetime of love.

Tyree was one of the good guys, or at least that's what Tynise thought. He grew up in the same building. They had gravitated towards one another over the years, watching each others backs, dodging the bums and addicts together.

"What, you gonna act like you don't know me now?" Tyree said.

"What's up Tyree," Tynise turned around and responded with as much cool as she could muster. "Ain't seen you around in a while."

"What's up?" Tyree nodded to Lauryn, Marisol and Ruby. "Yeah, I've been busy workin' on my thing."

"Your thing. What's that?" Tynise asked.

"Me and Damon been layin' down some tracks in our studio."

Tyree's eyes wandered from Ruby's legs, revealed by tight pink shorts to Lauryn's ample chest bursting out of a clinging t-shirt that said "party girl" to Marisol's bare mid-drift exposing a perfectly dimpled belly button. "What's up Lauryn? You still like to get your party on, huh?"

"Yeah, whatever. What kind of studio you got?" Lauryn asked skeptically. She still remembered how badly Tynise took it when she found out Tyree was seeing other girls behind her back.

"You know I've been working at the grocery store for a while now. I saved all my paper and Damon got some from hustling them DVDs. We got a tight studio hooked up at my place."

"You got all that studio stuff at your house?" Lauryn asked. "You just beggin' to get jacked."

"I ain't worried about that." Tyree pulled up his shirt to expose a gun.

"Is all that necessary?" Tynise looked at him with disdain.

She was surprised to see him with a gun. Of course, a lot of kids had guns, but Tyree was never like that. He always had dreams and a plan to get out of the hood playing it straight. That's what she liked about him.

"It's just for protection. I worked too hard for my stuff to get punked. You guys should come over and check it out."

"We might come by," Lauryn responded automatically, intrigued by anything that might break up the monotony of a boring afternoon.

"I have to watch my sister," Tynise replied throwing her eyes at Lauryn.

"Alright then, I'll check you later." Tyree nodded at the girls and walked away in his cool, smooth way.

Tynise stared at the ground. The other girls stood speechless for a moment. They all remembered how tight the two were. Whenever you saw Tyree, you saw Tynise right by his side. They even had their own nickname, TNT.

"It's okay, that boy ain't about nothin'," Lauryn broke the ice.

"I know. I ain't sweatin' that fool." Tynise lifted her head. "I don't know. It's so messed up, you know. How can someone be with you everyday, listen to all your problems, make you feel like you're all he needs, and then turn around and screw any other girl he can find that will do it with him?"

"Please, you know all boys are dogs. All they want to do is hit it and quit it," Ruby said.

"I don't know what you ever saw in that little boy anyway," Lauryn made a funny face like she was sucking on a lemon.

"Hey, Tyree may be kind of short and skinny, but it was more than that. He used to write me songs and stuff. I don't know. He just made me feel different."

"You know that's just part of his game," Ruby said rolling her eyes. "They will say or do anything to get what they want. I don't think I ever met a boy who really wanted to know about me."

"True that," Lauryn replied lifting her hand for a high five with Ruby. "I know when a boy is talkin' to me he ain't got but one thing on his mind."

"That's 'cause you don't give him nothing more to think about," Marisol commented. "You have to make him want you so bad he don't know what to do. If you just give it to him, he won't never come back. Why should he? You already give him what he wants. That's what my mama told me and I believe it. I still have Hector."

Ruby threw up her arms. "God, I wish you would stop throwing Hector in our faces. Don't you know he's like one in a million? Other boys don't act like Hector, okay. I tried what you're talking about. Remember Jamal? I thought he was so cool, you know. He listened to all my problems. That's something my parents never did. I wanted it to be real, you know, so I made him wait for three months before we did it. I thought he was so sweet to wait until I found out he was doing it with other girls behind my back the whole time he was making me feel guilty for having him wait so long."

All four stood silent for a moment. Each looked at the boys running up and down the court, realizing none of them would ever appreciate them for who they really were. Only Marisol found peace in her thoughts.

Ruby, Tynise and Lauryn simultaneously experienced a sinking feeling of worthlessness as they silently acknowledged the truth. Boys don't know what love is. They don't even really want to know. How could they understand the value of the one thing held most sacred and precious to any girl, her love?

"I don't know what to do," Tynise broke the silence. "But I'm sick and tired of these triflin' brothers messin' with me like it don't mean nothin'."

"Me too," Ruby agreed.

"I know what to do," Lauryn said boldly. "I'm gonna have a baby."

Silence fell upon the group. Each was in deep thought.

"It would be nice to have someone you know would always be there for you, no matter what," Ruby sighed.

"A baby would always love me, no mater how fat I got and it would never leave me for another mother." Tynise lamented. "Plus, I know I'd be a good mother. I've been taking care of my brother and sister since I was eight. I know how to take care of a baby."

"Me too, I helped my mother a lot with my brothers. I know what to do with a baby and I know Hector gonna make a great father. I wanna have a bunch of babies with him," Marisol added smiling as she did every time she imagined her future with Hector. She looked to Lauryn. "Are you really gonna do it?"

"I'm gonna do it. I know I can be a good mother. I ain't gonna be like my moms. I'm gonna love my baby."

"You ain't worried about taking care of it?" Tynise asked.

"I can get on the system, no problem. We all can. They hook you up with food stamps and you can always get W.I.C."

"You know, Lauryn, the government doesn't give you as much as they used to. It's not all that easy anymore," Ruby said.

"I don't care. I'll find a way. Girls do it all the time and they don't have no problem. Anway, I can always get my hustle on doin' hair. You know I got skills. Who knows, I might even get a chair in a shop or somethin'," Lauryn answered defiantly.

"So, you got it all planned out," Tynise said. "You've really been thinkin' about this, huh?"

"Damn straight. I know what I'm doin'. I mean, I know it ain't gonna be easy, but it'll be worth it. Think about it, your own baby to love."

"What about all the parties and fun you'll be missing out on," Ruby asked.

"What about it. I been hangin' out since I was twelve. I ain't gonna be missin' out on nothin'."

"I hear you," Tynise agreed with Lauryn. "What you gonna miss; the same old house parties, gettin' high, them boys pullin' at you like you a slab of pork ribs. It would still be hard though. My mother would kill me."

"What about college?" Ruby persisted. "You're gonna give up college. And you too, Mari, don't you still wanna go?"

"I can still go. Hector says all I have to do is keep my grades up. And I know my family will help. They gonna be mad at first, but they will help. Hector's parents, too. You know his brother is in college. Hector's the only one left at home. We can live there."

Tynise thought for a moment, "I probably won't be able to get into college anyway. It's not like my mother has a lot of money to send me to school, but I guess I can get financial aid. And you guys would watch the baby for me if I have class, right?"

"Damn straight. You know I got your back," Lauryn said smiling at Tynise.

Tynise continued, "Ruby, I don't think you have to worry about a thing. Your parents will probably hire you a nanny or somethin' to help you with the baby."

"That's true. Anna cooks, cleans and does everything else at home. I know she would help me. She loves babies." The corners of Ruby's mouth eased into a sinister grin. "My parents would lose their minds. Daddy would be so disappointed." She paused for a moment. "I'm gonna do it."

Lauryn held her hand in the air for Ruby to slap and turned to Tynise, "Are you in?" She touched Tynise lightly on the arm and looked straight into her eyes. "We can do this. We'll do it together."

"It would be nice, my own baby," Tynise responded in a shaky voice. "I'm in."

"Mari?" Lauryn asked.

"I wanna do it. I wanna have a baby with Hector."

"There it is." Lauryn's face lit up and a sparkle of hope rose in her eyes, Baby Club."

"What?" the others responded.

"Baby Club, that's what we are. Let's make a pact. We're all gonna have babies, we're all gonna stick together, and we're all gonna help each other out no matter what."

"Lauryn's right," Ruby said feeling more confident about the idea. "We have to have each other's backs, especially when it comes to our parents."

"Hey, I got a idea," Lauryn almost shouted. We should make a bet. I mean don't you think the first one who has a baby deserves a prize or somethin'."

"Okay, so, what should we bet?" Ruby asked.

"I know. For the first one who delivers, the other three have to do her homework for the rest of the year," Lauryn suggested.

"Uhm, I don't think so," Tynise laughed. "There's no way I'm goin' to college if you gonna be doin' my homework."

"True that," Lauryn laughed back.

"What about we take the winner out to a fancy dinner, you know at one of those expensive restaurants," Ruby suggested.

"Excuse me," Lauryn blurted. "What are we supposed to use for money."

Ruby's eyes fell to the ground. She was usually careful not to throw around the fact she had money. "I got it," Ruby exclaimed, trying to redeem her self. "We all have something in our closets the others like to wear, right."

"You know I love your Baby Phat jeans," Marisol said.

"Yeah, and I want them Apple Bottoms you got," Lauryn beamed.

"Hello," Tynise interrupted. "You know I can't get into none of your clothes.

"Maybe not, but you got some nice accessories," Ruby

suggested. "You know, that belt with all the different colored beads and all those great ear rings you have."

"That sounds okay," Tynise gave in.

"Then it's settled," Ruby said. "The first one to have a baby gets to pick out one thing from each of our closets, including accessories."

Chapter 7

Everyone liked to hang out at Marisol's. There was barely enough room inside the humble home to accomodate its residents, but the wrapped around porch provided the perfect chilling spot for the neighborhood kids. No matter how many, Marisol's mother welcomed all with open arms. Ruby never mentioned it to anyone, but she loved the family atmosphere. Marisol's was the perfect place to avoid the emptiness of her house.

Ruby's mother was usually too busy catching up on her "beauty sleep" or running to the country club to interact with her when she got home from school. The only meaningful contact Ruby had with anyone in the house was with Anna. Anna had a family of her own, but she ran Ruby's house like a well oiled machine. Even though mother treated Anna like she was just one of the help, Ruby, on a subconscious level, had grown to think of her as a surrogate mother.

Anna secretly resented having to leave her home before her own children woke up to take care for someone else's child, but nurturing instincts created a soft spot in her heart for Ruby. She was happy to help Ruby with her problems, but she knew better than to get too personally involved in the lives of her employers. As soon as she picked up Ruby from school in the afternoon, Anna was back on the bus headed for home. Anna never worked weekends so, for Ruby, the two hours spent with her in the morning was the only time the house felt warm.

Everyone had something to do after school that day, so Ruby ended up alone at the house. The uncomfortable solitude gave her too much time alone with her thoughts, with the feeling of sinking in quick sand. The only thought that brought her peace of mind was the bet. The possibility of a baby to care for when she got home from school inspired her to work her way out of the funk. She fantasized about holding her baby in her arms, holding it to her breast for feeding, even changing the diapers. Each thought brought her joy in a way she never considered before. Once she had the baby, she would be a woman; full, complete, and never alone again.

Ruby jumped up when she heard the phone ring, grateful for the opportunity for human contact. "Hello."

"Hey, Ruby, what's up?"

"Mari, where you been?"

"I had to visit my tia. She been real sick."

"You know, Mari, I've been thinking about the bet."

"Yeah."

"I think it's gonna be amazing, you know, having a baby."

"I know. I can't wait to see Hector again."

"It's gonna be so easy for you with Hector. You're so lucky. What am I gonna do?"

"It's not gonna be so easy. Hector don't want no baby."

"You don't have to tell him. You can just get pregnant."

"Yeah, but he always wears a condom. He's so careful, every time."

"So what are you gonna do?"

"I don't know. I'll think of something."

"Well, at least you're one step ahead of me. I don't even have anybody."

* * *

A few blocks away Lauryn and Tynise watched the boys playing basketball at the park. Tynise begrudgingly took her sister with her everywhere she went. It had been that way as far back as Tynise could remember. She didn't like it, but she understood. No eight year old child should ever be left alone in the projects.

Jasmine was the typical little pest. She buzzed around her big sister and eavesdropped on her conversations like a fly on a wall, soaking up her surroundings, hearing too much too soon.

"That's the one, right there," Lauryn said as if she were plotting a scheme.

"Let me guess, the tall one with the braids, right?" Tynise replied.

"You know it."

"You know he deals."

"Yeah, so."

"Why do you always go for the bad ones?"

"He ain't so bad. At least he can take care of my needs. I bet he takes good care of his kids. I wouldn't have to worry about diapers or nothin'."

"What makes you think he's gonna support you? How do you know he ain't like all them other brothers out there just hittin' and quittin'? My auntie says if you let a bad man plant his seed in you, your baby will turn out bad, too. And she should know. She got some crazy bad kids."

"He can hit it and quit it if he wants to. All I know is he better take care of his responsibilities. If he don't pay his child support, I'll take him to court."

"Hello, he's a drug dealer. You think he's gonna care about some court order? It's not like they can take money out his pay check."

"True that," Lauryn replied, disappointed at the hole in her logic but undeterred. "I gotta stick to my original plan and get me a ball player."

"That ain't gonna do nothin' for you either. I can't believe you think any of these fools is gonna make it to the NBA. It's just not gonna happen."

"Not true. What about Dre?"

"Okay, I'll give you Dre. He got some skills, but every girl in school is after him."

"Right, and he be hittin' all of them. Look, I know he ain't gonna marry me or nothin'. I just want his baby. When he makes it to the pros, that's when I'll hit him up for the child support."

"Dag, you got it all planned out, don't you."

"Straight up, my plan is tight, right?"

"I don't know, Lauryn. I'm lookin' for a boy that's gonna be around. Maybe I can find a boy like Hector. I don't know. I just know how hard it is for my mother. It's gonna be hard to do it alone."

"What you talkin' about, alone? I'm gonna be there and Mari and Ruby, okay. We're all gonna do it together, Tynise, remember that. But if you think Prince Charming is gonna come ridin' through the hood on a white horse and sweep you off your feet, baby, you the one trippin'."

Chapter 8

"B.C. on the prowl," Lauryn called out as she, Tynise, Marisol, and Ruby approached the park.

"B.C.?" Ruby asked.

"B.C., Baby Club," Lauryn laughed. "There goes Dre."

Lauryn took off across the concrete towards the basketball court where a group of three boys stood in a semi-circle. Her intent was clear as her hips switched from side to side. She didn't have the natural padding in the back a lot of the other girls had, but she knew how to accentuate an ample D cup. Naturally blonde hair made her unique in the hood. She wore it long, stretching half way down her back and she had developed a ritual of flipping, twisting, and bopping the blonde locks in a way that put the boys in a trance and made all the other girls jealous. Most of the sisters on the block secretly wished they were born with "good hair". Lauryn had the best hair on the block.

"What's up, girl?" One of the boys said as she approached, but Lauryn didn't reply. Her eyes were fixed on Dre with laser beam precision. She waited patiently for Dre to acknowledge her presence and lured him in by twisting her hair in her fingers and seductively sucking on a lollipop.

Dre played it cool for a moment, then turned to Lauryn. "I seen you around, ain't I? What's your name?"

"I'm Lauryn," she replied in her best, rehearsed, sexy voice.

Tynise, Ruby, and Marisol watched her from across the basketball court. They were used to Lauryn's routine.

"I think our girl's on roll," Ruby said.

"Yeah, you know it's on when she breaks out the lollipop," Tynise laughed. "That girl really knows how to work it. I could never be like her."

"I know," Marisol agreed. "How can she take all them boys looking at her like a piece of meat? Don't she know they only want one thing?"

"She knows. That's why she's acting that way." Tynise shook her head. "She wants Dre to be her baby's daddy. She thinks he's gonna make it to the NBA and she'll be able to hit him up big time for child support."

"Dre does have it goin' on," Ruby replied after thinking for a moment. "I hear the scouts are checkin' him out. You know, that might not be a bad plan. Ballers do get paid. Even if he doesn't make it to the NBA, he could end up playing in that European league or something. Those guys get paid too, not as much as in the NBA, but enough for her to raise a baby right."

"Not you, too," Tynise sighed. "Don't you even care if your baby has a father?"

"I care," Ruby snipped. "But fathers don't always stick around now do they?"

"No, I guess they don't," Tynise agreed.

"So, if I can't have the man, I might as well as have his money. I can give my baby all the love it needs by myself," Ruby said smugly. "I bet I could get Reggie if I really tried."

"Who's Reggie?" Marisol asked.

"You know Reggie, our running back. He's got pro skills, too. Everybody says so. Have you seen him this year? He got all buffed over the summer. He looks so hot."

"Okay, I know Reggie," Marisol said. "Don't he go with Trina? Hey, Ruby, you know you not supposed to go after another cheerleader's boyfriend."

"Whatever," Ruby rolled her eyes, "Reggie's a great football player. He's got a hot body, he's super fine with those light brown eyes, and he's smart too. I think he's an honor roll student. He's the complete package. I want him."

"There she goes," Tynise interrupted Ruby and Marisol. They silently watched Lauryn disappear around the corner with Dre. "When that girl makes up her mind to do something, she really goes for it."

That evening Tynise sat on a metal bench in front of her apartment building watching Jasmine jump double dutch with her friends. It took her back to when all she needed was a good round of double dutch to make her day complete. She hardly noticed the bums and addicts back then. She was completely focused on the silly rhymes they sang and the beat of her feet on the street, synchronized with the rhythmic slap of the rope.

Now, she had so much more to worry about. She had to cook dinner amost every night, keep up on her school work, and watch Jasmine, always watch Jasmine. She recognized every threat the streets had to offer. If she was able to let Jasmine play outside for a couple of hours without seeing something disturbing, it was a good day. It had been a good day up until now.

Tynise glanced across the street and noticed a disheveled woman stumbling in high heels over the broken concrete. She was moving as fast as wobbly legs could move. Her maroon colored wig shook and bounced as it barely hung on to a stocking covered head. She wore a bright, yellow, tight spandex mini skirt and black, fish net stockings that climbed up long legs. Tynise immediately recognized her as a pro even before she saw her pimp closing in on her. It didn't take long for him to catch up and begin with the slapping and scolding.

Tynise used to feel sorry for the slutty looking women with different color hair that walked up and down the streets. She wondered why everybody watched, but no one ever helped as the ugly men beat on them. It took a while for her to realize that the women were not really looking for any one to help. No matter how hard they were beaten, they kept coming back the next day. They

53

were hooked on something, drugs or the pimp's affection. Whatever it was, it was something Tynise didn't understand.

There was no need for concern this time. Jasmine was on one side of the street and the pimp had successfully controlled his situation on the other side. He wouldn't come her way.

Sunset was Tynise's favorite part of the day. She loved the way the sun turned the sky from blue to orange to red. It changed the complexion of everything it touched. If only for a few minutes a day, Tynise could look into the sky and pretend she lived in a colorful painting instead of a dark, gray concrete jungle.

"What are you staring at," Lauryn approached Tynise with a wide grin.

"Just the sky."

"Plannin' on an escape?"

"Every day," Tynise smiled.

"What's up with home girl?" Lauryn looked cross the street.

"Oh, she's just gettin' her daily beat down. What are you so happy about?"

"Me and Dre did it," Lauryn proclaimed, her face flushed with a sense of accomplishment."

"When?"

"Right now. I just took him back to my place. He didn't take long."

"Dag, Lauryn, first Jerome, now Dre. Who's next?"

"I don't know, but you better get on the stick or those big hoop earrings you got are mine. I got a good head start on you."

"No kidding. Jerome and Dre, all in a week. You better slow down. At this rate you ain't gonna know who the father is. You gonna end up like one of those girls on the *Maury Povich Show*, dragging in brothers from all around the hood to see who your baby's daddy is."

"It don't matter. I hope it's Dre's. You know he got good genes. My baby could make it to the NBA. And if it's Jerome's he'll be really tall and good lookin'. Plus Jerome used to play ball too, remember. Either way he's gonna have good genes."

"How do you know it's gonna be a boy?"

"I don't, I'm just sayin'. I don't care. If it's a girl she can go in the WNBA. They get paid, too."

"So, it's all about gettin' paid, huh."

"No, you know I'm gonna love my baby, no matter what."

Tynise and Lauryn talked about boys, babies and the "freaks" that walked the streets. They watched out for "home girl", but she must have moved to a street with more action. They swore to each other neither would ever end up that way.

Lauryn decided to spend the night at Tynise's. Lately, she had been sleeping there more often. It was better than staying by herself in her dingy apartment. Tynise's mom wouldn't be home until after midnight, so they had all the freedom they needed. Tynise just had to make sure Jasmine and Quincy were in before sunset and they had something to eat. Tynise knew how to cook, but she decided to make them a frozen pizza. Her mother usually left her some chicken or pork chops to fry or a big pot of home made beans. Mom was the queen of beans. All kinds of beans; lima beans, navy beans, baked beans, and of course black eyed peas, it didn't matter. She seasoned them so you could eat them all day and still want more.

Tynise was in charge when Mom was at work. Jasmine had not given her any trouble, yet. She was content playing silly games with her friends or just vegging out in front of the TV. Quincy, however, was getting harder to handle every day. She used to be able to intimidate him into listening to her, but he was eleven years old now and too big to push around.

He had learned his mother's schedule so he was there when she got home from work. He knew mother, tired from working a double shift, would soon be asleep. And he laughed at Tynise as he sneaked out the door to hang out with his friends all night. Many times Tynise had tried to tell mother about Quincy's night moves, but Quincy lied well and mother wanted to hear what she wanted to hear.

Lauryn usually slept on an old couch in the corner of Tynise's bedroom. Tynise and Jasmine still slept in the same bunk beds they had had for years. Everyone but mother knew Quincy would be gone for the night. Jasmine didn't mind, she got the living room couch and fell asleep in front of the TV. Tynise and Lauryn had the bedroom to themselves. They puffed on a blunt before they fell asleep, carefully blowing the smoke out the window. Tynise didn't smoke a lot, but she liked it how it helped her remember her dreams. That night she dreamt about Tyree. They walked together, hand in hand, through a beautiful forest filled with trees as tall as Chicago's highest skyline. They stopped for a picnic by a glistening waterfall and fed the deer and squirrels directly from their hands. Tyree bent to one knee and told her how much he loved her. Tynise slept with a smile on her face all through the night.

Chapter 9

The next day Tynise dragged Jasmine to the park hoping to see Tyree. She sat on the bench stretching her neck in every direction for a glimpse of the only boy who ever made her feel like a grown woman. She thought about how close she felt to Tyree then and how nice it would be if her baby's daddy was someone she actually had feelings for. Then the memories of his playing around surfaced. She remembered the hurt and wondered. *Is it still so easy for him to tell lies? Is it possible for him to make a change?*

Jasmine pulled on her sleeve, insisting that it was time to go back upstairs. Hours had passed by, but Tynise was too entranced in her daydreams to notice.

"Hey Ty." The deep voice Tynise remembered from her dream was standing behind her.

"You need to stop sneaking up on me like that." Tynise turned around to face Tyree.

"Where you been?" he asked.

"I've been around. You know I don't go nowhere. I have to watch Jasmine all the time. Where you been?"

"I've been around, too. I don't hang out like I used to. If I ain't workin' at the store, I'm workin' on my music."

"Yeah, you told me about that. So, you think you got skills, huh."

"We be throwin' down, Ty. You gotta hear what I be workin' on, it's tight, for real."

"I'm sure it is," Tynise said encouragingly. She felt obliged to acknowledge his enthusiasm.

"Why don't you and come up and check out the studio. Bring Jasmine with you."

Tynise tugged on Jasmine's arm and they followed Tyree. Jasmine complained at first, but she had to go where Tynise said.

Tyree lived by himself. His mother was a statistic, a chicken head, a crack fiend who would do anything for any amount of the deadly rock. They didn't talk about it much, but Tynise had always admired him for his ability to hide his pain and press on. He hadn't seen his mother in days. It was better that way. Any contact he had with her was just an unnecessary reminder of her painful existence.

Tryee should have been a statistic, lost to the streets, but he hooked up with a mentor at the Boys Club early in life. Max, a retired police officer, recognized Tyree's situation, his need for a father figure and his willingness to accept the help he needed. Max continued to be a steadfast influence over him. He got Tyree his job at the grocery store. Max was the only one Tyree trusted with his problems until he met Tynise.

"You gonna have to excuse the place." Tyree opened the door.

"It's not so bad." Tynise tried to conceal her disgust as she looked at a sink full of dirty dishes and watched the cockroaches scamper to safety. "Come on, Jasmine." She stumbled over empty forty ounce botttles and pizza boxes, but she hardly noticed the mess. Her eyes bounced from Tyree's lips to his deep, brown eyes, and she focused on his every word. She admired him, his struggle and she thought he had done well for being sixteen and practically living on his own.

"Ew, it stinks," Jasmine blurted out before Tynise could quiet her.

"Yeah, it's been a minute since I cleaned up."

"She didn't mean that," Tynise apologized. "So, where's your studio?"

58

"It's in my room. Come on."

He led them into a dark room with piles of clothes splattered all around and strange looking blankets hanging from the walls.

"What's with all the blankets on the wall?" Tynise asked.

"It helps to keep the outside noise from gettin' in when we're recording. The whole room is sound proof."

"What's all this stuff?" Tynise pointed to an elaborate display of blinking lights sitting on a table in the corner.

"That's where it all happens. I got a 24 track digital recorder, those are my monitors, this microphone can make any voice sound smooth as silk, and it all runs through this computer."

"This is tight, Tyree. How'd you get all this stuff?"

"I told you, Ty, I've been workin' at the store and saving my money. Max helped me plan it all out."

"Max, that old man has some serious knowledge."

"For real, he done set me straight on a lot of things."

"This is cool." Jasmine picked up a microphone and started to sing a funny little song, "Pickles and juice, pickles and juice, pickles and juice with chips on the side." Her feet stumbled over the thick cables that stretched out in every direction and she fell into one of the three foot tall speakers.

"Watch out, shorty," Tyree called out.

"Sit down, Jasmine, before you break somethin'. Dag, why I gotta take you everywhere I go anyway."

"She's okay. She can't break nothin'. I want you to hear somethin' I been workin' on."

He started pushing buttons and turning knobs. The computer screen lit up and the speakers emitted a strong, pulsating beat, filling the dark, drab room with life all its own.

Jasmine jumped up from the couch that Tyree also used for a bed and started to bounce up and down to the beat.

"Jasmine, I said sit down," Tynise snapped at her, but she knew she couldn't be heard over the thumping beat.

"Let her go, she's okay. Ain't nobody can sit still when I'm throwin' down beats. Check it out.

Alright, feels tight, make it right
Comin' at you like dynamite
You feel me
I'm for real, you can't kill me
Raised up in this hell, with the garbage and the smell
And there ain't no way I can see to break free
There ain't no angels lookin' out for me
I ain't got no moms, ain't got no pops
I'm just runnin' the streets gettin' caught up
In the game, in the game, in the game
It's all in the game

Got no shame
This is how I'm livin'
Doin' what I gotta do like a mega villian
Gotta take from the rich to feed the poor
You know the score
You know the deal
You know the way
You know the play
You gotta do what it takes to get by these days
In the game, in the game, in the game
It's all in the game

What do you think?" Tryee looked at Tynise with confident eyes.

"It's tight, real tight. I didn't know you could spit like that. You got a real strong voice, you know, like DMX."

"That was good," Jasmine shouted out. "Do another one."

"I can spit all day. I got a ton of raps, beats to go with 'em and everything."

They stayed at Tyree's listening to him lay down beats until they lost track of time.

"Is it nine already?" Tynise said looking at a digital clock on the wall. "We gotta go. Mom will kill us if we're not home when she gets there. She's already going crazy 'cause Quincy ain't never around."

"Let's go. I'll walk you back over there."

Tynise smiled at him, impressed by his kind nature. On the way back, Tynise told Jasmine to walk in front of them. Far enough so she wouldn't be able to eavesdrop on their conversation but close enough to keep an eye on her.

"I had a dream about you last night," Tynise confessed.

"Yeah, what about?"

"We was walking in this beautiful forest. There was deer and squirrels and all kinds of animals and stuff. It was wild."

"The forest, you must have been trippin'. I ain't never been nowhere near no trees and deer."

"Yeah, I know, it was just a dream."

"Can you hang out later?"

"I don't know. I can probably sneak out. My mom usually sleeps pretty hard when she gets off work."

"I'll be hangin' out. I'm a look for you."

"Okay."

Without thinking about it, Tynise put her arms around Tyree, gave him a deep kiss, and quickly ran away, afraid to face his reaction.

Chapter 10

"So, how long has it been since you were with those guys," Ruby asked Lauryn as they walked to Marisol's house after school.

"About two weeks."

"Do you feel any different?"

"No, I don't feel nothin'."

"Well, you'll know if you don't get your period. When does it come?"

"Around the third week, but it comes on different days."

"Then it should be coming up soon. I'm a trip out if you're pregnant."

"I know it'll be crazy. You better be ready to give up them Apple Bottoms."

"Oh, hell, no." Ruby shook her head.

"Hell, yeah, you know I got a good head start on you. Who you gonna get with?"

"I don't know. I don't have anybody."

"So, I ain't got nobody either. That never stopped me. All you gotta do is decide on which one you want and move in for the kill."

"You crazy," Ruby laughed. "I know all that works for you, but I don't think I could ever do like you do. I can't just put myself out there like that. I'm too shy."

"You don't have to be crazy with it. All you have to do is focus all your attention on him. Then break out a lollipop and it's over."

"Yeah, I've seen you do your lollipop thing. It does seem to work for you. Where'd you learn that mess anyway?"

Lauryn stopped for a moment to think. "I don't know, my mother, maybe. She's good at gettin' men. She don't know nothin' about keepin' a man, but she can always get one."

"Did she teach you that lollipop trick?"

Lauryn saw her mother in her mind, spread out on their couch, a sweaty man between her legs, a lillipop in her mouth and a solemn grin slithered across her face. "I guess she did. That's a trip. I never thought I was gonna learn nothin' from her. Don't worry, you can hook up at the party tonight."

"You know Reggie?"

"The football player?"

"Yeah," Ruby replied with a far away look in her eyes, "I'm really trying to get with him."

"I feel you, he's fine."

"I know he's gonna be at the party tonight, but I bet he's gonna have his girlfriend with him."

"That ain't nothin'. Just wait for her to go to the bathroom and jump in there and go for it. And don't forget your lollipop."

* * *

All the athletes, dealers and bangers were at the party, but it was hard to tell one from the other. Everyone, from the wanna to the true ballers, grew up in the same streets. Some were born with natural athletic talent. If you had skills, serious skills, everyone in the neighborhood had your back, vicariously living your dream. The non-athletes fought, hustled and developed different skills. Either way they could get their respect.

Marisol was cuddled up with Hector at the end of a long, black leather sofa. They shared the space with two other couples, but they didn't seem to mind. They were in their own little world.

"It looks like Mari and Hector are up to their old tricks," Ruby told Lauryn with a hint of jealousy.

"You know that. So, where's your football star?"

"I don't see him, but I know he's gonna be here."

"Hey now, look at that," Lauryn exclaimed. "Is that Tynise with Tyree?"

"I can't believe she took him back."

"I can. She's always had a thing for that boy."

Ruby looked disappointed. "Tynise has Tyree, Mari has Hector, and you've already done it with Jerome and Dre and whoever else."

"You tryin' me? Don't be tryin' me."

"What, I ain't lying."

"So, you don't have to say it like that."

"I'm just playing," Ruby could see Lauryn was getting upset. "But, for real, I'm gonna be the only one without a baby."

"So, what are you waitin' for? I'm sure any one of these guys would love to do it with you."

"I'm not gonna just do it with anyone, Lauryn. Oh my God, it's Reggie," Ruby blurted, then covered her mouth like she just let out her best kept secret.

"Where?"

"Over there, see." Ruby nodded toward his direction, trying hard to go unnoticed.

"Oh, yeah, I see," Lauryn smiled. "Who's that fine brotha with him?"

"I don't know, but I don't see his girlfriend anywhere."

"So, go talk to him."

"I can't go over there by myself."

"I'll go with you. You got your lollipop?"

They walked over to the boys with welcoming smiles and deliberate steps.

"Hey." Lauryn took the lead already working her lollipop.

Ruby timidly followed and nervously put her lollipop in her mouth. Reggie and his friend immediately ended their conversation and turned to the pair.

64

"What's up?" Reggie locked on to Ruby's exotic looking face, then, let his eyes cruise down admiring how her t-shirt and jeans clung to her bathing suit model body. "You're a cheerleader aren't you? I've seen you around."

"Yeah, I'm on the team." Ruby took the lollipop out of her mouth. "I'm Ruby."

"Reggie." He extended a hand for her to shake. "Nice t-shirt," It was a ready made excuse to look at her breasts. "Have you seen his new video?"

"Yeah, it's off the chain. Fifty Cent is crazy."

"What's up, Snow Bunny, I'm Derrick." Reggie's friend extended his arm to Lauryn.

"I'm good," Lauryn replied.

"Yeah, I bet." Derrick let his eyes travel up and down her body. Lauryn didn't seem to mind, but she didn't know that Derrick was the kind of guy who wouldn't care whether or not she minded.

Lauryn was wearing a pink t-shirt with a picture of a bright white bunny under bold letters that read, "Snow Bunny". The boys gave her that name years ago and it stuck for obvious reasons.

"Yeah, that's my nick name."

"I guess it is," Derrick reached out and ran his dark finger through Lauryn's long blonde hair.

"Yo, Derrick, Derrick," a voice called out from across the room.

"I gotta roll, shorty. I'll catch you later." Derrick quickly dropped his hand and rushed off.

Lauryn turned to rejoin the conversation with Ruby and Reggie, but Reggie was standing with his back to her. He was so tall and muscular that she couldn't even see Ruby standing in front of him. Realizing there was no chance of breaking into their conversation, she turned around to find a smoke filled room, booming music and couples leaning against each other mouth to ear. There was someone for everyone. Marisol had Hector, Tynise had Tyree, and, now, Ruby had Reggie. She sipped on her beer trying to figure out how, in a room full of people, she could feel so alone.

65

An uncomfortable feeling led Lauryn to a place where only a mental escape could ease her pain. She recognized a familiar scent and remembered the blunt in her cigarette case. She lit it, swayed carelessly to the music, and transformed into a secure, sexy woman that any guy would want. She scanned the room with new found confidence looking for her next conquest and found Dre standing in a group with a girl on each side. Their eyes met and locked. For a moment, Lauryn thought she made a connection, then she noticed Dre's eyebrows tighten and the corner of his lips turn into a frown.

She knew he was a player, but couldn't help the twinge of jealousy growing inside, making her brain turn hot. "He don't gotta play me off like that," she mumbled to herself, lowered her head, and took another puff from the blunt. The dizziness consumed her mind and she focused on the music trying not to lose her buzz.

Jerome nonchalantly walked by. He bumped into Lauryn and sent her stumbling backwards.

Lauryn opened her eyes. "Jerome, what's up? Where you goin'?" She grabbed his arm.

"Don't be pullin' on me," he snapped at her. "You don't know me like that."

"I knew you the other night, remember. What, you ain't got no time for me now? You can't talk to me? You could talk to me in the back of your Escalade."

"Get away from me. That wasn't talkin'. You wanted it, so I gave it to you." Jerome turned to his friend. "Man, that trick is crazy. Let's go."

"Hey, you said we was gonna hang out," she called out to him as he walked away.

Lauryn looked for Tynise, but she was still with Tyree. She couldn't stand to stay at the party. She hurried home, sunk into her couch and drowned her sorrows in beers and blunts. She found solace tripping on all the poor suckers on Jerry Springer whose lives were more messed up than hers.

Back at the party, Marisol whispered in Hector's ear. "You know it's gonna be our two year anniversary."

"It's been a great two years, baby," Hector replied, his head buzzing from the Corona. "Come on, let's dance."

"Really." Marisol was surprised. Hector usually never wanted to dance.

The song was strong and rhythmic with a booming pulse that rushed through their bodies like thunder. It took over their senses and commanded their bodies to rock, bounce, shake, and roll. It was one of those songs that made everybody want to stop what they were doing and groove to the beat.

Tynise and Tryee and Reggie and Ruby were dancing, too. Marisol, Ruby and Tynise glanced at each other and smiled. Everything was perfect in their worlds.

As if on cue each turned their backs to their partners and began gyrating their hips like they were auditioning for a gangster rap video. Ruby was the best dancer. For as long as she could remember she had bounced and grinded to music videos on BET.

"You know I have to be home by eleven," Marisol faced Hector and shouted in his ear. It was the only way she could be heard over the music.

"Alright, let's go." Hector recognized the hint. It meant he only had about an hour of messing around time before he had to get her home.

Hector didn't want to get on her father's bad side. They had a mutual respect for each other. Hector loved to hear his stories about the old gang banging days and Marisol's father relished the opportunity to share his knowledge with a kid who actually had a chance of making it. With all the gang activity in the neighborhood, he knew Marisol could do a lot worse than a kid who came from a good family, studied hard, played football instead of running the streets and planned on going to college.

They went to an empty parking lot behind the school. The back seat of Hector's Oldsmobile had plenty of room for their night moves. She was open to him in every way. She wanted his baby in the raw, instinctual way a salmon fights its way upstream to spawn. She waited for just the right moment, when Hector was so into it he wouldn't notice, and reached down to slip off his condom. When he was done, she pretended to take it off him and throw it out the window. At first she was afraid Hector would catch her deception, until she realized the Corona had a good hold on him. That night Marisol fell asleep stroking her stomach, dreaming about the future.

Chapter 11

"Is that Ruby?" Tynise tugged at Tyree's arm as they waited in line at the movie theater.

"That's her and she's with Reggie. When did that happen?"

"I don't know. I haven't heard much from Ruby over the past couple of weeks. Oh, but they were talking at Antonio's party, remember."

"Right and they was rockin' it pretty good on the dance floor, too."

"Lauryn told me Ruby really likes Reggie. Don't he go with that girl, Trina. He must not be too into her or he wouldn't be here with Ruby tonight, right?"

"Whatever you say, baby. That's Reggie's thing. It don't mean nothin' to me."

The theater was about ten miles away from the projects in the neighborhood with perfectly manicured lawns and more white faces than black. The twenty minute bus ride left too much time to stare out the window watching the landscape transform. Too much time to realize how much they missed not having the things most people took for granted. The ride there was bearable. They could dream about somedays and gonnabes as their eyes moved from the bitter, concrete streets to the clean, bright landscape where everything seemed so perfect. The ride back was not so easy. With each turn in the road the dreams dissipated and reality hit like a cold slap in the face.

"Hey, what's up," Tynise shouted out as Reggie and Ruby caught up with them. "Why didn't you tell me you guys were coming to the movies? We could have come together."

"It was just kind of a last minute thing," Ruby replied. "Reggie was just dying to see *Street Racer*."

"Awe man, *Street Racer*." Tyree's eyes began to bulge with excitement. "I hear that one has some crazy race scenes."

"Yeah, man, with motorcycles and cars," Reggie replied with mutual excitement.

"We're going to see *The Love Letter*," Tynise smiled at Tyree.

Reggie laughed at Tyree. "What's up, man, you whipped?"

"Naw, man, she just wants to see it, that's all," Tyree sneered back.

"Do you guys know each other?" Ruby asked.

"I've seen him around the way," Tyree said.

"I've seen you play football. You're pretty good," Tynise added, smiling at Reggie a little too long for Tyree's liking.

"Reggie." He extended his arm for Tryee to acknowledge.

Tyree looked at the hand and hesitated before giving it an obligatory slap.

"Reggie, this is my friend I told you about, Tynise," Ruby continued.

"Hey, Tynise, what's up." Reggie extended his hand again, this time to meet a soft, warm handshake. "Why don't you see *Street Racer* with us," Reggie suggested, prompted by an instinctual need to bail out a kindred brother who was forced to endure one of the biggest chick flicks of all time.

"That's a good idea," Ruby agreed looking at Tynise with hopeful eyes.

"I guess that would be okay." Tynise caved in. "But you owe me a movie pick." She nudged Tyree.

"I gotta go to the bathroom," Ruby said as they entered the theater. "Come on, Tynise, before the movie starts."

They burst through the bathroom doors bubbling with excitement about their new boyfriends.

"So, how long has this been goin' on?" Tynise giggled at Ruby.

"About three weeks."

"Don't he have a girlfriend?"

"Yeah, Trina, but he's not really with her. If he was he wouldn't be with me, right. He doesn't even see her that much anymore."

"But they do still see each other?"

"Sometimes, but I'm gonna put an end to that, watch and see."

"Okay, I hope you know what you're doing."

"Don't worry about me. I got it covered. What about your thing? You know Tyree's a dog."

"He's changed, I swear. He ain't like he used to be. He writes me raps and we go places. None of them other boys ever took me to the movies. It's nice to be with someone who has some money to do things."

"So, you think it feels right this time?"

"I think so."

"You did it with him, didn't you?"

"Not yet, Ruby, but I think I will tonight. My mom's working real late. I think I'm gonna give it up when we go to his place after the movie."

"How do you know he's not just gonna dog you out again."

"I don't, but it feels right. I don't know. At least I'll know who my baby's father is, you know. Tyree has always been there for me when I really needed him. He's a good guy. He really is and he has a good job so he can help out with the baby. I think it's gonna be okay."

"I can stay out late, too. We're gonna go to a friend of Reggie's house after the movie. His family is out of town and he gave Reggie a key so we have the whole place to ourselves. Tonight's gonna be perfect. I bet if I have Reggie's baby he'll forget all about Trina. Baby's mama always comes first, right?"

"I guess, but you know some guys get scared and don't want nothin' to do with you. I hope Tyree ain't like that."

Ruby paused to think for a moment then admitted, "I guess that's just the chance you take with boys."

* * *

Tynise looked at Tyree with love struck eyes as he made race car noises, turned knobs, flipped switches, and scratched a beat on a vinyl record.

"You really liked that movie, didn't you?" Tynise asked.

"How you like this old school?" Tyree ignored her comment and scratched on.

Tynise sat, almost hypnotized, relaxed and energized by the precision of rhythmic hands flowing across the turntables. She closed her eyes and let the beat flow through her.

Suddenly, Tyree stopped playing to ask Tynise a question. "What would say if I told you I wrote a song?"

"What do you mean? You write lots of songs. I like the one you played for me the other night."

"No, not a rap song. I mean a real song, you know, like Neo."

"I didn't know you did that kind of music."

"I can do it all, baby. Listen to this." He pulled a crumpled piece of paper out of his pocket, cleared his voice and began to sing.

"It's your time, it's my time, it's our time to be together
I've been waiting for someone like you and
You've been here all the time
I can still remember when we played in the park
You were scared and I was too
I always had your back and you had mine
So together we'll make it through
Me and you

I'm still working on it." Tyree paused, too nervous to lift his head from the paper. "It's called Me and You."

72

Tynise tried to speak, but the words got stuck in her throat. In his song, she finally heard the words she had been craving to hear all her life. It was like a dream come true.

"Do you like it?"

"I love it, Tyree. Is it about us? It is about us ain't it?"

"Yeah, it's about us."

"Do you really feel that way about me?"

"I guess," Tyree replied in a soft voice embarrassed to share his raw emotions.

"I really, really like it." Tynise moved closer to him.

They sat side by side on the couch he also used for a bed. She put her hand on his knee and squeezed. If there were any doubt left, the song had washed it all away. He was the one and this was the time. They fell into each other over and over again. The thought of using protection never crossed their minds.

* * *

"Step back. We don't want to let the dog out." Reggie told Ruby as he opened the door to the modest, but well kept two bedroom home."

"Dog?"

"Don't worry, it's just a little ankle biter. You could fit him in a purse."

"Oh, I bet he's cute. Where is he?"

"He's around here somewhere. He'll come out when he hears the food hit the bowl. I don't like that little rat dog anyway. I'm always afraid I'm gonna step on him."

The sound of tiny, scampering feet approached from around the corner the second he poured the food.

"Oh, he's so cute." Ruby bent down to pet the quivering fur ball.

"What the hell is he shaking for," Reggie snipped. "It's not cold in here."

"Leave him alone. He's so cute."

73

"Whatever." Reggie had more important things on his mind than the dog. "Dwyane said there should be some stuff here for margaritas. It should be in one of these cupboards." He rummaged through the kitchen slamming doors.

"Quiet. You're scaring the dog."

"Who cares about the dog? Come on, help me look. Never mind, here it is. I mix a mean margarita. Think you can handle it?"

"I can handle it."

Ruby's eyes took in every inch of Reggie's biceps and broad chest, bulging through a conspicuously tight t-shirt. She felt a flash of heat, all over, with each bend of his arm. Every pour of her body was ready to be touched.

"Thank you," she said in a soft voice and tried to ignore the slight tremble in her hand as she took the glass.

"You want to watch a DVD. Dwayne's got that tight surround sound."

"Sure."

"Go ahead and pick one out."

Reggie sat on a large, black leather couch and checked out Ruby as she stretched and bent to look at the DVDs stacked in shelves on either side of the TV.

"You know I always thought you were one of the prettiest cheerleaders."

"Yeah, but not as pretty as Trina, right?"

"I don't know about Trina, we've been on the outs lately."

"What do you mean?" Ruby sat next to him on the couch.

"I don't know. She don't understand me like you do, you know. It just seems like we fight all the time. It's really starting to get on my nerves. You and me never fight like that."

He moved closer to her, put his arm around her and looked into her eyes. She thought he was being romantic, but he was really looking for clues, trying to figure out if she was ready to go all the way. He didn't know Ruby had already decided tonight was the night. They started to kiss. Both got what they wanted from the other.

Chapter 12

Marisol had Hector, Tynise had Tyree, Ruby had Reggie, sometimes, and Lauryn had anyone who could provide a momentary escape. They saw each other at school, of course, but they had all been so busy with their boyfriends it had been about a month since they spent time at Marisol's.

"Baby Club in the house," Lauryn exclaimed.

"That's right, we are a club," Ruby said as she smiled at the others.

"I think I might have a baby," Marisol blurted as if the words would explode in her mouth if she held on to them one second longer.

"What do you mean?" Ruby asked.

"Me and Hector been doing it a lot. I feel different inside. I don't know."

"But do you have any symptoms, you know, like morning sickness? Did you get your period yet?" Tynise interrupted.

"No, no I didn't, not yet. And I been throwing up, but it don't just happen in the morning." Marisol smiled. "You think I might have a baby?"

"Wait a minute. I thought you said Hector likes to use protection," Ruby said.

"Yeah, how did you get Hector to do it without a condom?" Lauryn asked.

"I made it so he don't know," Marisol replied.

"What do you mean? What did you do?" Tynise asked.

"Hector don't notice too much when he drink a lot of beer. I just put my hand down there and take it off when we was doing it."

"You just took it right off?" Ruby asked.

"Yeah, he had too much beer to care."

"That's a good idea. I bet he didn't notice at all," Lauryn said.

"Yeah, and I seen this movie on TV. This girl, she put a hole in one with a pin. She say it works, so I try that, too."

"Did it work?" Tynise asked.

"I don't know. I think so. I do feel different inside. Like a real woman." Marisol gently stroked her stomach.

"I haven't had my period yet either," Ruby said looking more excited than worried. "Me and Reggie have been doing it a lot, too. I've been making him forget all about Trina. He never says anything about using a condom when we do it. I bet I'm pregnant, too."

"I ain't had mine either," Tynise smiled. Things been real good with Tyree, just like it used to be, only better. He don't even try to look at other girls now. He don't need to. We been goin' at it so much, he don't have the time to look at no other girls."

"I ain't had mine," Lauryn jumped in. "I just know I'm havin' a baby. I don't know who the baby's daddy gonna be, but I know I'm gonna have me a baby. Did I tell ya'll about Big Ced?"

"Who?" Tynise asked.

"Big Ced. You know, Cedric he's on the basketball team. They call him Big Ced."

"Oh, yeah, I know who you're talkin' about," Tynise replied. "Ain't he that really big, tall brother?"

"Yeah, but Big Ced ain't really that big, if you know what I mean," Lauryn giggled and the rest joined her in a good laugh.

"You're gonna make sure your baby's daddy plays ball, huh," Ruby said.

"True that," Lauryn agreed. "You know I be throwin' up, too, and my boobs hurt."

"Oh, that's a sign. Your boobs are supposed to hurt when you're pregnant and they get bigger, too. Are they getting any bigger?" Ruby asked.

"Not that I can tell, but they do hurt, Lauryn continued."

"Oh, I bet you got a baby." Marisol clapped her hands together in excitement.

"I bet we're all pregnant." Tynise jumped to her feet. "We need to find out for sure."

"We should all take one of those home pregnancy tests," Ruby suggested. "I hear they're real easy. All you have to do is pee on the strip and if it turns a different color that means you're pregnant."

"That's a great idea. Are they expensive?" Lauryn asked.

"I don't think so, but don't worry about that. I got some money from my allowance. We can all take one," Ruby offered. "We can get them at the drug store."

Ruby, Tynise and Lauryn sprinted off to the drug store, but Marisol had to stay at home to watch her little brothers. Her mother had taken Claudia and Belinda with her to the market, so they would be gone for a while and Papi wouldn't be home from work until later. The timing was perfect.

Marisol anxiously waited on the porch for the others to return. She hardly noticed the commotion her little brothers made racing toy cars across the floor. Her mind was consumed by daydreams of the picture perfect family she would have with Hector and the baby. She was fantasizing about all the cute outfits her baby girl would wear when she saw her friends running down the street.

"Did you get them, all four?" Marisol rushed to meet them at the porch steps."

"We got 'em." Ruby ripped open the bag and handed one to each of them. "Now, let's see. It says here all we have to do is pee on a strip. If it turns blue you're pregnant and if it turns pink you're not."

"It's my house. I get to go first." Marisol ran into the house and shut the bathroom door.

77

The other girls ran behind her and anxiously waited at the door.

"How long has it been?" Tynise asked.

"Oh, I can't wait," Lauryn slapped her hand against the door. Come on, Mari, what's takin' so long?"

They heard a toilet flush and Marisol jerked open the door. "I was so nervous. The pee wouldn't come at first."

"Here, let me see." Lauryn grabbed at her wrist to see the strip. "Has it turned colors?"

"I don't see nothing," Marisol said as they huddled around the strip. The only sound in the room was Marisol whispering prayers underneath her breath, "Dios mio, please, say yes, say yes, please, please."

Gradually, the strip began to turn color.

"I see something," Marisol shouted. "It's turning, see."

"Is it blue? I can't tell," Tynise yelled.

"I see it," Lauryn exclaimed. "It's blue, you see it, blue. You gonna have a baby!"

They all burst into joy dancing, bouncing, and shouting out loud.

"Let me go next." Lauryn peeled off her jeans as quick as she could and squatted on the toilet.

"Where's your other bathroom?" Tynise asked as she bolted out the door and frantically searched down the hall with Marisol chasing behind her.

"Hurry up, Lauryn." Ruby stood impatiently over her with a test in her hand.

Lauryn quickly peed on the strip and held it up to the light.

"Come on, get off the seat. It's my turn," Ruby insisted.

Lauryn stumbled off the toilet, her jeans still around her ankles. Her eyes remained focused on the little strip. She held it up to the light over the sink, hoping the key to her happiness would soon emerge.

Ruby finished peeing and stood beside Lauryn in front of the sink. Both held their strips to the light. They were so caught up in anticipation they almost forgot to pull up their jeans.

"Is that Tynise?" Lauryn said responding to the sound of footsteps in the hallway. "Come on, let's go."

Ruby and Lauryn ran down the hall to meet Tynise and Marisol coming out of the other bathroom. They faced each other in a circle under the light in the middle of the hallway. Each stared at the strip they held shaking in their hands. The air was still except for the sounds of heavy breathing and whispered prayers.

"Mine's turning, Lauryn suddenly shouted. "God, please let it be blue."

Even the sound of breathing stopped as they collectively willed the color to change.

"Mine's changing, too," Ruby screamed.

"It's blue, it's blue," Lauryn called out dancing and jumping for joy.

"Mine's blue, mine's blue," Ruby yelled and joined Lauryn in her joyful dance.

Tynise's strip was still changing color. She clutched it in her closed hand, afraid to see the result. Lauryn noticed her staring at her closed hand and ran to her side.

"Let me see, let me see," Lauryn grapsed at Tynise's clenched hand as Ruby and Marisol joined them.

"What are you waiting for," Ruby asked. "Let's see."

"I don't know. I guess it just didn't seem real before. I'm nervous now," Tynise replied.

"There ain't nothin' to be nervous about," Lauryn said as she put her arm around Tynise. "If yours is blue, then we'll all be pregnant together, just like we planned. Come on, let's see."

Tynise slowly opened her hand to reveal a blue strip.

"Yes," Lauryn shouted. "I knew it. We're all gonna have babies at the same time. It's perfect."

"I hope I have a girl," Marisol said. "I can teach her how to cook and do make up and do her hair and nails."

"Me too," Lauryn interrupted. "I'm gonna be such a good mother to my baby. She's gonna love me forever."

"I don't know," Ruby said. "I think I want a boy. He's gonna be my little man and I'm gonna teach him the right way to respect women. He'll grow up to be a beautiful, strong man. What about you, Tynise?"

"I think I want a girl, but it really don't matter," Tynise answered inspired by the camaraderie of her three best friends. "I'm gonna love my baby no matter what."

"The first time you did it did you ever think you could have a baby?" Ruby asked the group.

"I don't think about that then," Marisol replied. "Me and Hector been together for eight months before we do it. I make him wait so long he say he was gonna explode. That's what he say to me all the time. He say it gonna explode or fall off if he don't use it. I remember we wait until his parents go out and we do it in his bed. It hurt, but I love him so much I was happy with it."

"Tyree was my first," Tynise smiled at the memory. We were both fourteen. I trusted Tyree, you know. We was always real tight Everyone else was doing it and I wanted to know what it was like."

"I remember that," Lauryn interrupted.

"So, how was it?" Ruby asked.

"It was okay, you know," Tynise replied. "It wasn't what I expected. It was over before it started. You know what I mean."

"I know what you mean," Ruby sighed. "They make such a big deal out of it, but then it's over just like that." She snapped her fingers. "Rodney was my first. He was a white boy from my old school. I thought he was cool at the time. He wrote raps and his beats were pretty tight. I didn't know he was a wanna be until I started hanging down here. Anyway, I was fourteen, too. I guess I wanted to know what it was like too, but it wasn't all that. I was just glad to get it over with."

"I was so wasted my first time I ain't know what was goin' on." Lauryn looked like she wanted to get something off her chest. "It was at a party. There was three of them. I don't know what happened. I must've passed out and they." Lauryn choked on the memory. "We was drinkin' and smokin', you know. God, that was some strong stuff, but I was gonna prove I could hang with them."

"How old were you?" Ruby asked.

"I was twelve, but my girls was already blowin' up." She looked down at her breasts. "I looked at least fifteen."

"How old were the guys?" Ruby continued.

"I don't know. They was all in high school."

"How come you never told me?" Tynise lifted her head to help her wipe the tears.

"I don't know. I didn't want noone to know, but it don't matter." Lauryn threw back her hair determined to move on. "It's just gonna be me and my baby from now on, and you guys, of course. Baby Club in the house."

Chapter 13

November brought in a soft chill, but nothing could deter the spirit of Lauryn, Marisol, Ruby and Tynise. They took the bus to the library after school. Each felt like they were in a different place from their dreary surroundings. They had a mission in life now. The mundane worries of project life, high school, and absent parents no longer carried any weight. They were focused and determined young women.

"So, this is what a library looks like," Lauryn laughed. I never thought I'd step foot in this place. Look at all these books."

"Duh, it is a library. What'd you expect?" Ruby giggled at her. "Come on; let's find a book on pregnancy."

Ruby went straight to the computer, punched a few keys and guided the others to a large section of books about pregnancy.

"How you know your way around here so good?" Tynise asked.

"We used to come here on field trips when I was at my old school. It's not that hard to find a book once you know how to look for it." Ruby picked up a thick, hard cover book. "It says, *Your Pregnancy, Step By Step*, this looks like a good one." The girls gathered around her as she browsed through the book. "Let's see, it gives you a step by step beak down of what our bodies will be going through from week one to week thirty six. This is perfect."

"What's it say," Marisol said, unable to contain her excitement.

"It tells you what's gonna happen to your body, what the baby is going through, what you should eat, and it gives you tips on things you should and shouldn't do. It has everything. Look, it says you're not supposed to have caffiene."

"Really," Tynise said looking surprised. "Guess I gotta cut out the Pepsi."

"Aye, me too," Marisol echoed.

"Okay, we'll definitely get this one and this one looks good, too. *Everything You Need to Know About Pregnancy From A to Z.*"

"Hey, look at this one," Lauryn held up a flimsy paperback. "It's, *The Official Book of Baby Names.*"

"Cool, we'll get that one, too," Ruby approved.

"I know if I have a boy I gonna name him Hector Jr.," Marisol said.

"Surprise, surprise." Ruby laughed

"No, really," Lauryn rolled her eyes. And what if it's a girl? You gonna name her, Hectina?"

They all laughed at Marisol's expense.

"Whatever," Marisol snipped back. "I'm hungry."

"Me too," Ruby agreed. "Let's go get a slice. I'm buying."

"I heard that," Lauryn added. "Ain't that place, Sal's, around the way from here? It's been a minute since I had a good slice."

"Oh, yeah, I could really use a thick, gooey slice. They have the best pizza there." Tynise glanced at her friend's slim waist lines then looked down at her own. "Now I got a reason to be fat. I'm eatin' for two."

"I still can't believe we all havin' babies at the same time," Lauryn smiled.

"I know. Its crazy," Tynise replied as her face turned solemn. "My mom's gonna trip."

"Mine's gonna trip, too. She's gonna be, like, so worried about what her country club friends will think," Ruby said in her best preppy girl imitation.

"Mama and Papi gonna be so mad. Mama had me at sixteen. She always tell me not to do like she do and wait for when I get older," Marisol said.

"Yeah, mine had me at seventeen," Lauryn said looking down at her feet. "All she's gonna say is I told you so. She's always complainin' about how she missed out on her best years 'cause of me."

"That's messed up," Ruby commented.

"You know," Lauryn continued, "ain't like I asked to be born. I ain't gonna get no help. She told me if I ever had a baby I was gonna have to raise it own my own. She said that's what she had to do and she ain't have no help. She always says if I'm woman enough to lay down to have one, I should be woman enough to raise it."

"What's your father gonna say, Ruby?" Marisol asked.

"He's gonna flip out, but I haven't even seen him in over a year. The baby will be half way grown by the time he gets back from Iraq."

"I just hope Hector not gonna be too mad." Marisol fretted. "I don't know what gonna happen if I don't have Hector."

"Please, you ain't got nothin' to worry about. That boy has a good heart," Tynise said confidently. "I think Tyree is gonna be there for me, too. He's always had my back and he's been so great since we got back together."

"I'm afraid to tell Reggie," Ruby contemplated. "I think he's starting to forget all about Trina, but I don't know."

"You know boys. If you tell him, he's gonna run back to Trina so fast the only thing you gonna see is the dust flyin' off the back of his shoes," Lauryn warned. "I ain't tryin' to fool myself. I know none of them boys I been with is gonna be there for me, but that's cool. I can wait and they gonna pay when they start makin' some real money."

"I don't know, Lauryn," Ruby interrupted. "Reggie can be pretty sweet when he wants to be. Maybe he'll want to be part of his kid's life, especially if it's a boy. God, I hope it's a boy."

84

"Well, you can think what you want, but I ain't countin' on no one but me to raise my baby," Lauryn retorted.

"Oh, that pizza smells good." Tynise breathed in a deep sniff as they waited in line for a slice.

There was always a line at Sal's. It was one of those traditional pizza stands that served up the thick, square slices Chicago was famous for. The conversation halted as soon as the pizza arrived. All four were consumed by the chewy crust, thick cheese and Sal's secret sauce that made it taste different from any other slice in town.

"Oh, that was good," Lauryn said as she wiped the last bit of sauce from her face and instinctively reached for a cigarette.

"What the hell are you doin'?" Tynise slapped her hand. "You can't be smokin' while you're pregnant. Everybody knows that."

"Please, one cigarette ain't gonna make no difference," Lauryn argued.

"Yes, it will," Ruby jumped in. "I remember this show I saw on the Discovery Channel a while back. It was all about the effects smoking, drinking and drugs have on a baby. You're not supposed to do any of that junk. You're baby could end up all messed up. It could be born premature or get fetal alcohol syndrome or be retarded. All kinds of bad stuff can happen. It could be as bad as having a crack baby."

"Aw, man, you don't want that," Tynise cringed. "My cousin, Laverne, was hooked on that crack when she had her baby. Jaquan's cute and all, but that little boy is all jacked up. You should see him. He don't never sit still and he can't even think right. Laverne said he can't even go to school 'cause he can't stop runnin' around the class, beatin' on the other kids. He gotta go to special classes."

"That's just cause she was a fiend," Lauryn stood her ground. "It ain't like I'm a crack head or nothin'. A cigarette or a beer or a blunt every now and then ain't gonna hurt nothin'. I bet my mother was drinkin' when she had me and I turned out okay."

"Maybe, but you do have a hard time in school, concentratin' and stuff." Tynise glared at her best friend. "I ain't sayin' you retarded or nothin', but you never could pay attention in class. You know what I mean. Don't you want your baby to do good in school?"

"Yeah, but..."

"There ain't no but, Lauryn. You can't be doin' that junk, none of it," Tynise scolded.

"That's right," Ruby agreed. "Don't you want to have a healthy baby?"

"Let's make promise to each other that none of us will do any of that stuff while we're pregnant," Tynise suggested. "No beer, no wine, no weed, no cigarettes, no nothin', okay."

"Okay," Marisol quickly agreed.

"I'm in," Ruby said.

"Lauryn?" Tynise asked.

"Okay, okay, I won't do nothin' no more."

"For real, Lauryn. I'm serious, and no caffiene," Tynise insisted, holding out her hand.

"I said okay, dag." Lauryn handed her the cigarettes and pouted for the rest of the evening.

* * *

The next day, Lauryn didn't show up at school until lunch time. She was wearing a pink t-shirt with large, cursive, black letters that read, *Baby Club*. Ruby, Tynise and Marisol sat at their usual table with blank expressions on their faces as Lauryn approached.

"What do you think?" Lauryn asked, grinning from ear to ear. "I got one for all of us, here." She reached in a plastic bag, pulled out three identical t-shirts and threw one to each of them.

"I think you lost your mind," Tynise barked, hiding her t-shirt under the table. "I'm not ready for everyone to know. You know I ain't even told Tyree yet."

"I didn't tell Hector yet either," Marisol squeaked in a nervous voice as she looked over her shoulder.

86

"You better not be going around telling every one we're pregnant," Ruby said. "I've got to be very careful about telling Reggie. And I don't want all my business out in the streets."

"Why not? You ashamed? You shouldn't be. Do you guys realize we're the first girls in school to get pregnant this year? We should get, like, a prize from the principal or somethin'."

"Quit playin', Lauryn. I'm serious," Tynise warned. "You better not tell nobody 'til we tell you it's okay. You could ruin everything."

"Okay, okay, I'll shut up about it. I just wanted somethin' to say we're all in this thing together, you know, like sisters."

Mark Miller

Chapter 14

Thanksgiving at Tynise's was always an event. As far back as she could remember, she had been allowed to stay up late the night before the big event and help with all the slicing, dicing and preparation needed to make everything go smoothly. Everybody was going to be there; Tynise, her mom, her brother and sister, her aunt from Wisconsin with her three kids, and Lauryn. But the only one Tynise was really looking forward to seeing was Tyree.

Her mom wouldn't be home until after eight. Thanksgiving was a big day at the diner, too. They opened the doors to feed the homeless. Tynise used to go down and help out, but now that she was old enough to cook, she stayed at home to make sure everything was done just like mama trained her. She may have been overwhelmed by all the kids running around their cramped apartment, but her Aunt Jocelyn was there to help. Jasmine helped clean the beans and even Qunicy helped by setting the table. Things had been boiling, simmering and baking all day, but no one touched a crumb until Tynise's mom got home at eight.

It was the kind of comfortable family atmosphere she dreamed of when she saw herself with Tryee and the baby. The feeling grew stronger when she noticed Tyree playing video games with her six year old cousin. Tyree had just met the kid, but they were playing together like he had known him for years. The scene touched a warm spot in her heart, but she couldn't help questioning herself as a wave of trepidation overcame her.

What if he don't want nothing to do with the baby? What if he denies it's his? What if he accuses me of sleeping around and calls me a whore?

Such negative thoughts ran through her head all day. One moment she felt happy, inspired by the comfortable family atmosphere and the next she was holding back tears, overcome with worry. The confusion was so overwhelming she had to find some space of her own. Tyree found her outside leaning on a car in front of the apartment building.

"What's up, boo? Everybody's lookin' for you." Tyree gingerly approached her.

"Nothin', nothin'," Tynise replied wiping the tears from her eyes.

"What do you mean nothin'? You cryin'."

"Really it's nothin', just stupid girl stuff."

"Are you sure? Is someone messin' with you? Who is it?"

"No, Tyree, really, don't sweat it."

"You know I'll tear up anyone who even thinks about messin' with you."

"I know." Tynise smiled and felt better. "You look like you was havin' fun playin' video games with my cousin."

"Yeah, he's a great kid. He don't like losin', but he takes it like a man."

"So, you like kids?"

"They alright, I guess."

"I bet you'd make a great father," Tynise said hoping to test the waters.

"Kids are cool. It might be tight to have a little shorty runnin' around some day."

The words ignited a spark inside Tynise. Her secret was on the tip of her tongue.

"But I ain't thinkin' about that right now," Tyree continued. "I gotta get myself straight first. I'll be graduatin' next year and I ain't got nothin' lined up but the grocery store. It's a good job and all, but I ain't plannin' on spendin' my whole life workin' there. I can't be thinkin' about no kids right now. I gotta work on my music. Gotta get that straight first."

Tynise heard what she wanted to hear. Tyree said he wanted a baby. The thought to tell him came to her mind, but only for a moment. Mom would be home in a few minutes and the drama of baby news would surely ruin a good Thanksgiving.

* * *

On the other side of town, Ruby had Thanksgiving dinner at the country club with her mother. She hated it. Besides the banquet waiters and bus boys, hers was the only brown face in the room. She was trapped in what she disdainfully called "white land". From the old ladies that wore too much make up attempting to disguise the effects decades of drinking, smoking and over exposure to the sun had on pale skin to the fat belly, balding, old men who laughed too loud at their own jokes, there was nothing she liked about the place.

Ruby excused herself from the table saying she had to walk off her meal. It was a believable excuse after eating a heavy, traditional Thanksgiving dinner. She had green beans, candy yams, cranberry sauce, cornbread and two big slices of turkey straight off the breast with a pile of mashed potatoes and oyster dressing covered in mushroom gravy. It was so good she could almost forget her hatred for anything so blatantly traditional, but food wasn't the problem.

Ruby concentrated on the clink of knives and forks trying to ingnore the relentless, mundane conversations. It might have been bearable if they were talking about anything interesting, but all they ever talked about was the latest toys they bought or the vacations they took. Ruby found herself walking alone through the hallways, wishing she was anywhere else.

"Ruby," a voice called at her from around the corner. "Hey, Ruby, I thought that was you. What you doin' here?"

"B.J., what's up?" Ruby answered relieved to see a familiar, brown face. I didn't know you worked here."

"Just tryin' to earn some extra cash. I almost forgot you was from up here. Don't tell me you belong to this wack club."

"My parents do. My mother dragged me down here for Thanksgiving dinner."

"I never would've pictured you with this crowd."

"Trust me, it's not my choice. I'd rather be hanging out with Marisol and them. She's cooking over at her place."

"My grandma's got a plate waiting for me when I get off work. That woman can burn. I can't wait." B.J. glanced at his watch. "Man, I gotta get back in a few minutes. You know they be workin' me like a slave up in here. They be losin' they minds if you come back late from your break. At least I can go back happy." He reached in the inside breast pocket of his yellow bus boy jacket and pulled out a small blunt. "You want to go outside for a smoke?"

"I wish I could, but I have to go back in there and I don't wanna smell of it," Ruby said thinking of her baby. In fact, there was nothing she would've liked more than to get her head numb before dealing with the old phonies again, but she was determined to do the right thing for her baby.

"Ruby," a shrill voice suddenly interrupted their conversation. "Ruby, what are you doing out here with him."

"We're just talking, mother, okay? This is B.J. He goes to my school. He's on the basketball team."

"Oh, nice to meet you, B.J.," she flashed a practiced smile. "Ruby, I need you to come back to the table. Dr. Johnson has some great advice on how you can get into Yale. You know he's one of their most influential alumni."

The last thing Ruby wanted was to go back to that table, but she wasn't in the mood for an argument. "See you later, B.J." She begrudgingly submitted to the request.

"Later, Ruby, I'll see you at school. Nice to meet you, ma'am."

Ruby's mother returned the courtesy with another phony smile and quickly turned to lead her daughter back into the dinning hall.

Mark Miller

Ruby survived the rest of the evening nodding in agreement to unsolicited advice and brandishing her own fake smile.

"Wasn't that nice of Dr. Johnson to agree to write you a reference letter? A letter from the Director of Neural Surgery at Memorial Hospital is priceless. His reputation is impeccable." Ruby's mother beamed on the car ride home.

"That's nice," Ruby responded rolling her eyes.

"So, who was that boy you were talking to?"

"I told you. He's just a boy that goes to my school."

"Is he in a gang?"

"No, mother. You know, not everybody that goes to Lincoln is in a gang. For your information, he's an athlete, not a gang banger. He's on the basketball team, he makes good grades and he might even get a scholarship to go to college."

"I hear they'll give scholarships to almost anybody who can play basketball these days. What does that say for our higher education system?"

"Whatever." Ruby sneered at her mother. "For your information, he's actually a pretty smart guy. He's an honor roll student and he takes the bus all the way down here just to earn some extra money to help out his grandma at home. That sounds pretty responsible to me. You just don't like him 'cause he's from the hood."

"It's not that, Ruby. It just wish you would associate yourself with a better class of people."

"What do you mean by that? And what do you call class anyway? It doesn't make you a good person just because you have money. B.J. has more character that any of these little country club boys running around here. He's a good student, a good athlete, and he works to help his family. I think I should respect that more than some punk, rich kid who's never had to work for anything a day in his life. Don't you think so?"

"I didn't mean it like that."

"Yes you did. Why don't you just admit it? You're a snob."

"Look, Ruby, I don't want to argue with you. It is Thanksgiving after all."

92

There wasn't much conversation for the rest of the ride home. Both mutually recognized they didn't understand each other and left it at that.

The first thing Ruby's mother did when she got home was pour herself a tall gin and tonic and retire to her bedroom. For the rest of the night the only sound Ruby heard from her was the clinking of ice into her glass and the sweet, melancholy harmony of Billie Holiday emanating from her bedroom. She figured her mother must miss her father more than she would let on. Besides all their differences, Ruby missed him too and wondered how any woman could marry a man who was away so much. He had been deployed for almost two years now. When he did come home, it was only for a few months and he was off again. Ruby promised herself she would never marry a man who would leave her alone with nothing but regrets and a bottle of gin to drown her sorrows.

If only Anna were there to keep her company. Of course she was having Thanksgiving dinner with her family. There was nothing o do but sit on the sofa, channel surfing. She daydreamed about Reggie, the baby and their future life together.

She stumbled across a show on teenage pregnancy about the hardships, commitment and the financial responsibilities of raising a child.

Ruby looked around at the thousands of dollars of modern art draping the walls, the collection of elaborate porcelain vases from various Asian countries, and the huge fifty inch HDTV in front of her and realized, as she snuggled into the cushions of a very expensive Italian leather sofa, that money would not be a problem for her. Besides, she would have Anna there to help. And if that wasn't enough she would talk her parents into hiring a nanny.

Finishing school wouldn't be a problem either. There was no way her parents would let her drop out of school and skip out on college. That would bring ultimate shame and they would do anything to keep the country club crowd from knowing they didn't maintain the perfect little family.

Mark Miller

The show, intended to scare teenagers into realizing the hard realities of getting pregnant so young, had the opposite effect on Ruby. She was more convinced now than ever that she was doing the right thing. She just had to figure out how she was going to tell Reggie and her parents.

Chapter 15

Marisol's, Tynise's families didn't have the money for stacks of presents piled under a tree; nevertheless their parents did the best they could to make it feel like Christmas. They decorated the house with lights and put up a modest tree that was nicely adorned with ornaments they had collected over the years. The kids were grateful for whatever their parents put under the tree. Everyone knew money was too tight for luxuries, even at Christmas. They considered themselves lucky if they got a winter jacket to fight off the chill or a new pair of shoes.

Lauryn wasn't so fortunate. Her mother had always found some excuse to ignore the holiday all together. This year she was in Atlantic City with a man she believed would be able to boost her career as a "dancer". She said she would be back in a few days, but Lauryn knew better than to count the days when she went away.

Aware of her situation, Tynise's mother developed a soft spot for Lauryn and treated her as if she was one of the family. There was always at least one present for Lauryn under Tynise's tree.

No matter how tight the money was they could look forward to a great meal. It was always turkey for Thanksgiving, and ham at Christmas. The tradition for New Years was collard greens, black eye peas, macaroni and cheese, and corn bread. Tynise's mother said the greens stood for money and the black eye peas were the change.

It was supposed to bring you money in the New Year. It had not worked yet, but they still believed.

Marisol's family had a different tradition for Christmas. Instead of ham, greens and black eye peas, they made tamales. It was her grandmother's recipe passed down to all the Mendez women. While the boys and men lay sprawled across the couches in the family room watching whatever soccer or football game they could find on TV, the Mendez women gathered in the kitchen to learn the tradition. They boiled corn and grinded it on a smooth, flat rock. The beef, seasoned with tomatoes onions and chilies, was shredded into fine, thin strips. Then it was carefully placed in the grinded corn that had been meticulously kneaded into soft, sweet dough. It was all wrapped up in corn husks that had been soaked in water for softening.

Ruby usually got anything she wanted for Christmas, but she would trade it all in for a room full of relatives sharing family traditions like this one. She wondered if Anna was doing the same thing with her family and wished she hadn't taken most of her vacation this time of year. Ruby was accostumed to an empty house at Christmas. Mother, as usual, had disappeared into her country club activities. She filled the void by spending most of her time at Marisol's. She loved the closeness of family and the sisterhood of her best friends and she learned how to make the tamales. She just had to be careful not to wear her new Gibrauds or show off the Prada bag she got for Christmas.

"I never have so much help in the kitchen," Marisol's mother commented. "We gonna have tamales for everyone."

"Yeah, mama, and we gonna have more help coming. Tynise and Lauryn gonna be here soon," Marisol said as she diligently tied a small piece of string around each end of a corn husk before putting it into the pot to steam.

"Aye, nina, no," Marisol's grandmother complained as she grabbed Ruby's arm. She shuffled close to Ruby and lightly slapped her hand. "Like this." Her wrinkled fingers, gnarled by arthritis, shook as they tied a perfect knot around the end of the tamale. She was a sweet, old lady, but she didn't play when it came to the tamales. She took great pride in making sure each one was prepared perfectly and would spend the next few days comparing them to last year's batch, fishing the family for compliments.

"Somethin' smells good up in here," Lauryn said as she and Tynise entered the kitchen.

"We making tamales," Marisol's mother welcomed them. "Come, let me show you."

Marisol, her mother, grandmother, sister, three cousins, Lauryn, Tynise, and Ruby were all crammed in the small kitchen, but no one minded the lack of space. Each had a job to do and contributed equally to the effort. Together they formed a synchronized assembly line. Every now and then one of the guys broke away from the game and tried to sneak a tamale, but grandma quickly shooed them away. Not until they had made enough for everybody would grandma assemble the entire group around the pile. She led them in prayer and the feast began.

Everybody had a plate full. The men and older boys sat around the TV watching the soccer game, the women sat around the table in the kitchen with the smaller children, and Marisol, Ruby, Lauryn, and Tynise lounged about Marisol's room, each with a pile of tamales stacked on their plate.

"Man this junk is good," Lauryn mumbled the words through a full mouth. "You call 'em tamales, huh. The bread is so sweet and the meat's kickin'."

For a few moments all you could hear was the chomping of jaws.

"Man, my stuff is sore." Out of nowhere Lauryn grabbed her breasts. "They're huge now, too. I can't even sleep on my stomach no more."

"Mine are getting bigger," Marisol said excitedly. "And they hurt, too."

"Don't worry, that's normal," Ruby reassured them. "I read it in the book we got from the library. They're supposed to get bigger.

They're getting ready for breast feeding. Mine are growing, too, but not as much as yours. What about you, Tynise?"

"Oh, yeah, mine are definitely growin'," Tynise replied. "Why you think I be wearin' all these big sweaters? They were big enough to begin with, but now it's gettin' ridiculous."

"I just hope I can keep these tamales down. I've been puking my guts out," Ruby said as she shoved another one into her mouth.

"I know what you mean," Tynise said with a concerned look on her face. "They call it morning sickness, but I be runnin' to the toilet all day and sometimes at night, too. I don't think that's right, is it? I think I should go see a doctor or somethin'. I don't want nothin' to happen to my baby."

"I throw up a lot, too. I think my mama gonna start asking questions. What we gonna do?" Marisol was just as concerned as Tynise.

"That's normal, too," Ruby said. "Morning sickness can and does happen anytime of the day or night, but I see what you mean. My mother would probably get suspicious to if she were around the house long enough to notice."

"Maybe we should go to a doctor or the clinic or somethin'," Lauryn said. "There's a lot of things we need to know."

"I know, but they gonna tell our parents? I don't wanna tell yet," Marisol said.

"Well, we gotta tell 'em sometime," Lauryn added. They're gonna find out anyway, you know, when we start to show."

"Lauryn's right," Ruby agreed. "We all have to go to a free clinic or something. The book said there's these vitamins we should all be taking and I bet there's a bunch of other stuff we should be doing that we don't know about. We don't even know when our babies are due."

"She's right. I ain't havin' my baby come out all messed up," Lauryn said.

"Okay, so we need to find some kind of clinic or somethin'," Tynise concluded. "We'll all go together. We're gonna do right by our babies, no matter what our parents say or do, okay."

98

"Okay," they all agreed.

"I wanna know my due date," Lauryn said.

"Well, let's see." Tynise started counting on her fingers. "The first time I did it with Tyree was round the last week of October."

"Remember, I tell you I take the condom off Hector. I think it was, like, Halloween." Marisol tried to remember.

"The first time me and Reggie did it was around that time, too," Ruby determined. "What about you Lauryn?"

"I don't know. It's hard to tell," Lauryn replied looking embarrassed.

"What, you didn't keep a score card?" Tynise teased.

"Very funny," Lauryn smirked back.

"It sounds like we all got pregnant at the same time. Let's see November, December, January...," Tynise started counting on her fingers again. "It'll be nine months in July. It's gonna be tight to see who wins the bet."

"It's gonna be close, for real," Ruby said looking at Marisol. "You know I'm gonna take your Baby Phats."

Chapter 16

Marisol spent a lot of time at Hector's now that he had the house to himself on weekends. With an older brother half way through college and a good plan in place for Hector, his parents had begun to take full advantage of their mid-life crisis. They had just enough left over from the money they had carefully set aside over the years to buy their dream Harley Davidson and joined the other weekend warriors, catching a second wind, cruising around the lake.

Marisol immediately took over the kitchen whenever they had the house to themselves. She felt very comfortable in his mother's apron, pretending as if she and Hector were already married. Tonight she was making two of Hector's favorites, pozole and chicken enchiladas. She wanted Hector in a good mood when she broke the news. A favorite meal might smooth the waters.

"Baby, this is your best pozole yet," Hector declared. "It's even better than my mama's, for real."

"Thank you, I'm glad you like it."

She took pride in pleasing Hector and felt confident she would be a good wife to him and a good mother to their baby. Her hands were sweating under the table. She was fearful of his rejection, but the look of satisfaction on Hector's face helped her realize there was no better time to tell him.

"Hector." Her voice barely squeaked past her lips.

"Yeah baby," he replied without looking up from his plate.

She could have waited until he finished eating, but it was much easier to talk to the top of his head than look him in the eye.

"I need to tell you something."

"Uh huh."

"I'm gonna have a baby."

"Yeah baby, I know, you want lots of babies. What was it, five or six or something?" Hector chuckled back at her.

"No, Hector. I'm gonna have a baby. I have a baby in me right now." She looked down and rubbed her stomach.

"What? No way. No." Hector jumped to his feet and began pacing around the room.

"Please, please, don't be mad. I'm sorry, Hector."

"No way. You can't be. No way. I know I used one every time we did it. I did. I know I did."

"I know, baby, I know. I don't know what happened. Please, don't be mad. It's okay."

"It's not okay. I'm not ready to be a father. I'm supposed to be going to college next year. What am I gonna do about that?"

"You can still go. You can go to college here in Chicago."

"You got it all planned out, huh. You think it's gonna be so easy. It's not. I always wanted to go away to college. I wanted both of us to be able to get away from here. How are we gonna do that now?"

"We gonna find a way, Hector." She felt confident enough to approach him and grabbed both of his hands. "We gonna have a good baby." She leaned her forehead on his. Her face was so close he could feel her breath on his lips. "Don't you want us to be together?"

"What does being together have to do with having a baby? It's too soon. We don't have to keep it, you know. You could get rid of it."

Marisol looked at him with sad eyes, "How you gonna think that, Hector. It's not a thing. This is your baby inside me. You want to kill your baby. Is that what you want?"

101

Marisol had a way of bringing Hector back to his morality and he immediately regreted his words. "Of course not, I'm sorry. I'm just not ready for a baby. Do you know how hard this is going to be?"

"I know, but we can do it. I know we can. My mama and papi gonna help and so will yours."

"I don't know about mine. There's no way they're gonna give up their weekends on the bike to raise some kid."

"Not just some kid, Hector, su nieto. They will love the baby just like they love you."

"I guess that's true." A slight smile creeped on to his face. "I'm gonna be a father, hey."

"Si, papi. Are you happy? Say you are happy so we can both be happy together."

"I guess. I don't know. I never expected nothing like this could happen to me."

* * *

Ruby woke up to the familiar sound of Anna stirring around in the kitchen. It didn't take much to rouse her from a restless night of tossing and turning, thinking about how she was going to tell her mother and Reggie about the baby. Most of all she was concerned about what her father would think, even though he was thousands of miles away. The anxiety had worked its way into every pore of her body. She had to tell someone before she exploded. As she wondered what Anna was making for breakfast, she realized a nonjudgemental ear was available.

"Good morning, Anna." Ruby couldn't help but smile when she smelled the aroma of her famous huevos rancheros. Anna's cooking was comfort food to Ruby, the perfect thing to make her feel at ease.

"Buenas dias," Anna grunted back as she methodically prepared Ruby's lunch.

Anna hardly ever smiled at work. She saved that part of herself for her children and husband. Nevertheless, she could often sense the loneliness in Ruby and always tried to have a kind word for her.

"I make your favorite today."

"I know, Anna, thank you. You know I love your huevos rancheros."

"Your mother leave a note for you on the refrigerator."

Ruby somberly walked across the room to retrieve her daily instructions from Mom. Notes left on the fridge were her favorite form of communication.

"Ruby, I'll be at the club until after eight tonight. Anna will leave you dinner. Love, Mom." Ruby smirked as she read the note out loud. "No kidding, it's not like she would ever have dinner with me or anything."

"Ruby, don't be so mean."

"What, you know I'm telling the truth. She would rather spend all her time at that stupid club than spend any time with me. Why does she hate me so much?"

"She don't hate you. She loves you. Only she don't know how to show it. It's not so easy for her."

"Oh, yeah, she's got it really hard living in this big old mansion."

"It's more to life than money. She's been without her husband for so long. It's not easy for her."

"So, I've been without my father. You think it's so easy for me?"

"No, of course not. I know it's been very, very hard for you. You're a brave girl."

"I mean, why can't she be down here eating breakfast with us right now? She could if she wanted to, couldn't she? She'd rather sleep half the day away and booze it up with those hags down at the club."

"Ruby, shhh, you not supposed to talk about your mother like that. She might hear you."

"So what? Do you really think she's gonna care?"

103

"Please, don't say that, Ruby. I do care." Ruby's mother appeared at the bottom of the stairs.

"No, you don't." She turned abruptly to face the object of her anger.

"Yes, Ruby, I do."

"No, you don't. Don't say you do when you really don't," Ruby responded to her calm, sorrowful voice with a rage that had been building inside for years. "How could you even say that? You don't know me. You don't even want to know me."

"Ruby, that's not true," she replied almost sobbing.

"That's not true, that's not true. Shut up," Ruby shouted back.

Respect your mother. Don't talk back. Be a good girl. None of the lessons her father tried to drill into her over the years mattered now. She was mad and Mom was going to know it.

"Ruby, that's enough," Anna intervened.

"What, Anna? You know she don't care. She's never here. She's always putting down my friends. Did you know she thinks if you don't have any money, you're worthless? She does. Ask her, she'll tell you."

"Ruby, please," her mother pleaded.

"No, mother, let's get it all out."

Ruby paused for a moment as if the rational side of her brain had an emergency braking system. Too late, the irrational side was on over ride.

"I'm pregnant."

"What?" Both her mother and Anna replied with popping eyes and dropping jaws.

"It's true. I am. I'm gonna have a baby."

"No, Ruby, no," her mother cried out as she lamented her dreams of Ruby graduating summa cum laude from Yale, making partner at one of Chicago's top law firms before she turned thirty, and giving her three beautiful grandchildren sired by one of Chicago's most eligible bachelors.

"Yes, Mother."

"Anna, could you please leave the room."

104

"She don't have to leave. I want her here. She's here more than you are."

"Yes, ma'am." Anna gave Ruby a sympathetic smile and eased out of the room. She knew better than to bite the hand that fed her.

The two stared at each other with tears in their eyes. Neither knew how to break the silence.

"I'm keeping my baby," Ruby blurted, inspired by a sudden motherly instinct.

"Ruby, I don't think you know what you're getting yourself into. You're not ready for a baby. Something like this could ruin your life. You have to get an abortion."

"No way. I knew I shouldn't have told you. You want to kill my baby? No way. No way."

"Ruby, think about your future, your plans. Oh, my, God, your father is going to be so disappointed."

"Please, who cares what he thinks."

She couldn't stand to be around her mother one second longer.

"Where are you going?" Her mother shouted behind her.

"Leave me alone. Baby killer."

Ruby retreated to her room and turned up her stereo to the most hard core rap station Chicago had to offer. The rebellious lyrics strengthened her resolve. Nobody was going to stop her from having this baby.

Downstairs Ruby's mother poured a gin and tonic, her answer to all the world's problems. She knew it was early, but the news gave her the perfect excuse to take a drink, just to calm her nerves, of course.

* * *

Marisol couldn't wait to share the good news with her best friends the next day at school. Ruby was the first one she saw as she searched up and down the hallways before class started.

"Ruby," Marisol ran up to her with a great, big smile on her face, "guess what?"

"Hey, Mari, what's up?"

"You not gonna believe it, Ruby. I tell Hector last night."

"What? You told him. What'd he say?"

"Let me tell you. First, I make him his favorite enchildas and pozole. He was eating so good."

"I don't care what you made him for dinner. How'd you tell him?"

"I wait 'til he is so into his food he can take anything I tell him and I just tell him."

"Well, what'd you say? I wanna know word for word."

"I just tell him. I'm gonna have a baby."

"Just like that?"

"Yes, just like that."

"Oh, my, God, what'd he say?"

"He get mad at first, but I think he gonna be okay with it. He start making a plan already. He say we can live with his parents until he finish college. He gonna go to college here and when he graduate he gonna have a good job and we gonna move out of the city in a real nice house." Marisol was in bliss as she laid out her plans with Hector. "He say he might be good enough to play football and get a scholarship at the city college and he say he know his grades are good enough to get a scholarship just for doing so good in school."

"He does have it all planned out, huh? I'm so happy for you, Mari." Ruby gave her a hug. "You're so lucky to have a guy like Hector. My mother wants to kill my baby."

"You tell her already?"

"Yep. She thinks I should get an abortion."

"Oh, Ruby. I'm so sorry." Marisol tried to consol her and raised her hand to wipe the tears from her eyes. "She didn't mean it."

"You don't know my mother. She doesn't care about anything but money and status. She's like this evil, heartless beast."

"I'm so sorry, Ruby. I know my mama and papi not gonna like it, but they not gonna wanna kill the first grandbaby. Que horrible."

Chapter 17

Usually, Tynise couldn't remember her dreams, but a grin slipped across her face as she awakened and recalled hersef and Tyree living in a beautiful two story home nestled in a typical suburban neighborhood. The stench of piss and stale alcohol was replaced by the aroma of flowers and freshly cut grass. Instead of gun shots and sirens, she heard chirping birds, buzzing insects, the laughter of children playing, and the funny circus music of an ice cream truck as it passed by. Alone with Tyree and their new baby daughter, she just knew raising a baby was going to be a breeze. Afterall, she had been looking after her brother and sister since she was a little girl.

She got ready for school feeling disappointed that it was just a dream, but thinking about Tyree left her with a warm feeling and a smile that restsed peacefully on her face all day. She floated through class with her head in the clouds, had lunch with Tyree and convinced herself that he was the one. Still, she didn't have the nerve to tell him. The day had been too perfect to spoil with risky news.

Tyree had plans to work on music with a client after school. Tynise would rather they spend the time together, but she didn't mind. She was impressed at how all the wanna be rappers paid for his beats and to use his equipment. She liked the way he called them clients and how seriously he took his music, like it was a real business. He was hard working and he had a plan. She just knew he was going to be a great father.

She had a couple of hours alone in the apartment with her blissful thoughts before she had to worry about Jasmine or whether Quincy was coming home or running the streets. She nearly jumped off the couch when a phone call interrupted her daydreaming.

"Tynise." An excited voice was on the other end.

"Hey, Mari, what's up?"

"You not gonna believe what happen."

"What?"

"I tell Hector," Marisol practically screamed into the phone.

"Told him what?"

"You know what."

"You told him?"

"Yes, I tell him."

"No way. What'd he say?" Tynise was screaming now, too.

"Aye, he get crazy at first. He jump up and start walking around real fast. He get mad, too. I can tell 'cause he be moving too fast, like he don't know what to do with his hands. But I take his hands and calm him down. I tell him everything gonna be okay. He gonna go to college here in the city and we gonna be together."

"So, he's okay with it?"

"I think so. He started to smile when I call him Papi."

"And what about you? You still goin' to college?"

"Yeah, I'm gonna go. Hector says we gonna get scholarships. And his parents gonna help us with the baby. They already tell us we can live with them."

"And he's really okay with it, for real?"

"For real. We gonna be okay. I'm so happy. I been looking for you all day at school to tell you, but I don't see you nowhere."

"I had lunch with Tyree. Then I just went straight to class."

"You been spending a lot of time with him. Is it better this time? Is he different?"

"I think so, but for real this time. He's great. We be hangin' out a lot together and I ain't even seen him look at another girl. He be helpin' me with Jasmine, too. He's great with kids. He's gonna be a great father."

"You gonna tell him?"

"I want to. I got to some time before I show, right? I don't know what to say. Everything's been goin' so good. I don't wanna ruin it. What if he gets really mad?"

"I know, but it's probably gonna be the best time to tell him, you know, 'cause everything going so good now."

"You might be right. So, how'd you tell Hector? I want to know exactly what you said, word for word."

"First, I make him his favorite dinner, enchiladas and pozole, He love it. His mama and papa leave us alone with the house all day. You know, like me and Hector was already married."

"That sounds perfect. So, when did you tell him? What'd you say?"

"I tell him when he was eating. I just tell him. I say, Hector, I have something to tell you. I'm gonna have a baby. I got a baby in my stomach right now."

"You told him, just like that and he didn't freak out?"

"Oh, he freak out at first, when he jump up and I have to hold his hands, but, after that, it was okay. I think he gonna like being a papi. So, you gonna tell Tyree?"

"I guess I have to. You think he'll be like Hector."

"That's for you to tell me. Does he love you?

"I don't know. How can you tell?"

"I know Hector loves me."

"How do you know?"

"Mama tell me when I first start to see Hector that if a boy really loves you he gonna do for you sometime. He not just gonna think about whatever he want all the time. He gonna show you that he be thinking about you. You know what I mean?"

"I feel you, I think. It's like when Tryee calls me before he goes to sleep at night. He says he likes my voice to be the last thing he hears at the end of the day."

"Like that, little stuff, you know. Mama says a woman can feel it if it's for real. Can you feel it with Tyree?"

"I can feel it. I think."

"Then tell him."

"You're right, I'm gonna tell him. Thanks, Mari, but I gotta go. Jasmine just walked in and I gotta cook dinner."

"Okay, Ty, good luck."

Tynise filled her mind with happy thoughts as she fixed dinner. She tuned out all the negativity coming from *The Jerry Springer Show* Jasmine was watching. She wouldn't let herself think about where Quincy might be and why he wasn't on the after school bus.

She borrowed Marisol's idea and decided to make something special for Tyree. Her mama's famous fried chicken should do with some butter beans, greens and corn bread. There were some greens in the freezer left over from Christmas and Mama always kept beans and corn bread mix in the house. Mama was saving the chicken for Sunday dinner, but Tynise used it anyway. Her mind was too consumed with Tyree to care.

Tynise thought about her dream last night as she walked over to Tyree's with a large paper bag full of chicken and all the trimmings. She conjured a fantasy where Tyree had the perfect reaction to her news and they all lived happily ever after in her suburban dream house. She knocked on the door happily anticipating seeing him again, but her patience turned to frustration when it took a while for Tyree to answer.

"Oh, hey, baby. What you doin' here?"

"What took you so long? What was you doin' in there?"

"I was sleepin'. I ain't hear you knockin' for a while."

"Well, you gonna let me in," Tynise grinned at him as she walked through the door without waiting for an invitation."

"Hold on, baby, slow down."

"What's up?"

"Nothin's up," Tyree answered with shifty eyes.

"What's that noise?" Tynise responded to the sound of movement in his room.

110

"What?"

"It's comin' from your room."

"There ain't no noise, baby, you trippin'. What's in the bag?"

"Oh, you want some of this, huh?" Tynise replied playfully, teasing him with the bag. "It's just some fried chicken, butter beans, greens, and cornbread, that's all. I shouldn't give you none since you made me wait so long."

"Aw, come on, baby. You know that's my favorite."

The smell of freshly fried chicken relaxed Tyree, but his eyes still shifted from Tynise to his bedroom door.

"Yeah, I know, sit down. You're so lucky to have me. You really don't deserve all this. You know that, don't you?"

"Yeah, baby, I know. You're the best. It's been tight, us hookin' up again. There ain't nobody like you, boo. You know that."

Tynise smiled as she anxiously prepared his plate waiting to hear the words that would make her dreams come true.

"You mean that, Tyree."

"You know I do. Ever since we was shorties, it's like we was supposed to be together. You know what I mean."

"Yeah, I do." His words made her feel light and heavy all at once. She sunk into her seat as she set the plate in front of Tyree.

Marisol was right, Tynise thought as she watched him, perfectly content, greasing on a chicken leg. *This is the best time to tell him. He knows we was meant to be together. He must love me.* Just as the words began to pass through her lips, she was interrupted by the noise coming from Tyree's room.

"Tyree.....What was that?"

"What?"

"Please, don't tell me you didn't hear it that time. What's comin' from your room? Who's in there?"

"It's just a client."

"A client, you said you was sleepin'," Tynise flared. Driven by womanly instinct, she rushed into the room.

"I...I...I don't want no trouble with you. I don't even know this fool that good," A tall, thin, light skinned girl negotiated as she

111

stumbled backwards across piles of clothes and CD cases. She could see Tynise's jealousy seeping through her pores.

This girl was everything Tynise was not, bulging in all the right places out of skin tight jeans and an even tighter t-shirt.

"I can't believe this. You been messin' around on me. I thought you changed. What am I gonna do now?" Tynise rambled outloud to herself. "I can't believe it. I can't believe I'm havin' a player's baby."

"What'd you say?" Tyree asked as Tynise walked towards him fuming and mumbling to herself.

"Oh, I'm out of here." Tyree's guest darted out the door.

"You heard me. I'm pregnant, fool, with your baby."

"How you know it's mine? Who else you been with?" Tyree snapped at her, pacing back and forth with his hands on his head.

"Who the hell do you think you talkin' to?" Tynise snapped back. "How could you ask me some mess like that? I ain't like you. You know I ain't been with nobody."

"I don't know nothin'. How I know it's mine? I ain't tryin' to be no daddy."

"What you mean you ain't tryin' to be no daddy? You sure was tryin' to get some. What'd you think was gonna happen? I didn't have this baby by myself."

"I don't care. I want a blood test."

"And what if it's yours? You ain't gonna be there for us?"

"I don't know. You can't just throw all this on me. Let's just get the test, okay. Damn."

The lack of support shocked Tynise speechless. She ran out the door asking herself questions. *How could I be so stupid? How could he cheat on me again? Why did I trust him again? How could he talk to me like that? How could he think I cheated on him? Does he really think I'm a slut? Why can't he be more like Hector? This ain't supposed to happen. We was supposed to be together. He's supposed to be down for me. He's supposed to hug me and tell me everything's gonna be alright. How could I be so wrong?*

112

Chapter 18

Ruby was upset about her mother, but she had grown accustomed to handling things on her own. She ws used to giving herself pep talks to push through the problems her parents were too preoccupied to acknowledge. She had inherited the leiutenant colonel's stubborness. Her mind was set on having a baby, and she believed positive self talk had the power to grant her dreams. *You can do this. You have your friends. You don't need her anyway. Me and Reggie are tight now. He's gonna be cool with it. Hector handled it good and so will Reggie.*

With a renewed sense of confidence, she decided to tell Reggie at school. It would be nice to cook him a good meal, like Marisol did, but she realized her limitations and she regretted refusing all the times Anna offered cooking lessons.

If nothing else, Ruby was a realist and smart enough to know why Reggie liked her. She checked herself in a full length mirror admiring her snuggest fitting jeans and a bright pink sweater that drew Reggie's eyes like a moth to a porch light whenever she wore it. She was on a mission. There was no way he could resist her best ammunition.

She spent the quiet car ride to school practicing what she was going to say in her head. Anna had made herself a promise not to get between Ruby and her mother, so she didn't mind the quiet, but she genuinely cared about Ruby. She couldn't resist giving advice.

"I was sixteen when I have my first baby," Anna broke the silence. "It's not gonna be easy for you. You gotta be strong now, for you and the baby. You not gonna have to do it alone, Ruby. I'm gonna help you. It's gonna be nice to have a baby in the house."

"Was it really that hard? What was so hard about it?"

"Aye, so many things. The baby gonna be crying all the time, all the time. Remember, three things make a baby cry. If he's hungry, he gonna cry or if he's sleepy or if you gotta change the diaper or if it's too hot or too cold or it's too much noise in the house, so many things."

"I thought you said there were only three things."

"I guess I lie," Anna replied with a smile.

"That's not funny. This is gonna be really hard. It's obvious I won't be getting any help from Mom. Did you know she wants me to have an abortion?"

"No, Ruby, she wouldn't want that."

"Yes, she wants to kill my baby just to save the shame of having a pregnant teenage daughter."

"Dios mio," Anna gasped and lifted her hand to her mouth as if the news had taken her breath away. She knew Ruby's mother was distant, but she had no idea she was so cold. No words could express sadness she felt for Ruby.

Ruby was still thinking about her mother when she left the car, but she found enough consolation in Anna's sympathy to keep her confidence high. Marisol's cheerful grin boosted her even further.

"Hey, Ruby, how you feeling?"

"I'm good. You look happy. Hector must be close by. How you guys doing?"

"He's great. What about you? Did you tell Reggie yet?"

"Not yet, but I'm gonna tell him today."

"Really. What are you gonna say?"

"I guess I'm just gonna tell him, but I have to get him to myself. He's always hanging out with his friends."

114

"Hey, whats up?" Lauryn bounced up on them. "You guys seen Tynise. She wasn't at home this morning."

"I haven't seen her," Ruby replied.

"Me neither, but guess what, guess what," Marisol interrupted.

"What? Dag, girl, calm down," Lauryn scolded.

"Ruby's gonna tell Reggie today."

"Are you really?" Lauryn asked as they walked down the hall.

"Yeah, I think it's time," Ruby hesitated.

"What you gonna say?" Lauryn asked.

"I'm just gonna tell him, that's all."

"Oh, you gonna get the chance right now," Marisol blurted, pointing to Reggie.

He was surrounded by his crew in their usual position, huddled around Reggie's locker. Ruby felt good when she saw the irresistible smile that made Reggie the center of attention wherever he went. She took pride in knowing she was with one of the most popular boys in school. She hadn't noticed from a distance, but as she approached she spotted Trina standing right next to him. A tightness formed in the pit of her stomach, her hands started to sweat, and her heart beat raced a mile a minute.

"Come on, Ruby, let's go." Marisol tried to coax her away, but it was too late. Instinct had kicked in and the voice in her head told her to fight.

Reggie didn't flinch when he saw her approaching. He looked Ruby right in the eye, giving her a moment of connection, a glimpse of hope that they were together. The moment quickly faded when Reggie callously turned to Trina and gave her a big, wet kiss on the mouth.

Ruby felt a tingling sensation that sped to her head in a rush of fury. Pregnancy had her hormones on overdrive and the switch had been flipped.

"What, you think you can just look me off like I ain't nothin'," Ruby exploded on Reggie from across the hallway.

115

"Who you think you talkin' to?" Trina snapped back at her as Reggie smiled. "You ain't nothin', trick. What, you thought you had somethin' goin' with my man, please. Get the hell outta here."

Ruby stepped closer. "Your man. Oh, he's your man, right? Then maybe you can tell me why I'm havin' your man's baby? What about that?"

"What, please, that ain't my baby," Reggie smirked at her. "You need to go somewhere with all that. How I know that's my baby? Who else you been with?"

"I ain't been with no one. You know that."

"I don't know nothin', you hooker," Reggie replied laughing at her as he slapped hands with his boys.

Tears rolled down Ruby's eyes. She was too overcome by betrayal to stop them, her pride too hurt to care.

"You heard him, trick, it ain't his," Trina barked at Ruby. "Get your sorry butt outta here."

"Who you callin' sorry? You ain't nothin'," Lauryn said as she stepped toward Trina like she wanted to fight.

"No, Lauryn, your baby." Marisol stopped her, placing a hand on her stomach.

"I know that's right," Trina taunted them while Reggie and his friends continued to laugh. "You pregnant, too, ain't you? What, you gonna say my man's your baby's daddy, too. All you tricks is pathetic."

"You ain't gonna be talkin' all that mess when the test comes back. Your man's a dog, but that's okay. He's gonna have to pay for his baby. He ain't nothin' and you ain't nothin'," Lauryn yelled at them as she, Ruby and Marisol walked away. It was the best she could do to save face.

Chapter 19

Ruby feverishly wiped the tears from her cheeks, but she wouldn't allow herself to cry too long before the lieutenant colonel's hard nosed training surfaced. He had always wanted a son and never seemed to notice Ruby was a little girl. She was his little soldier. He had taught her tears never solved anything. She knew; never let your enemy see you weak.

"He called me a hooker. That punk called me a hooker? Who the hell does he think he is?" Ruby sneered as she stomped down the hall.

"Don't be sweatin' that fool," Lauryn consoled.

Ruby tried to relax, but her brain was on fire. She could still hear their taunts echoing down the hallway. "He don't know who he's laughing at."

"I'm sorry." Marisol put her arm around Ruby and squeezed. "That's a mean boy. You don't want no mean boy. Not for you and the baby. He's no good for you."

"That's right, we don't need that fool. We got each other. We gonna be all the daddy our babies need." Lauryn pushed open the heavy steel doors leading outside and yelled, "Baby Club in the house."

"Is that Tynise?" Marisol pointed across the street. "Hey, Tynise."

Tynise pretended not to hear. She had been filtering out voices all day; her head in a daze. She had so many fantasies that Tyree would be there for her. Like a boxer stuggling to survive a standing eight count, the reality of his reaction had set her off balance.

"Tynise, over here." Lauryn sensed something was wrong as she watched Tynise cross the street. "What's up Ty?" she asked with a sympathetic voice.

Tynise stood in front of her three best friends ashamed to lift her head. "I told Tyree," she whispered.

Ruby gravitated towards Tynise, put her arms around her and said, "I know. I just told Reggie." They held each other tightly. "I know. I know. How could I be so stupid?"

"I caught him doin' some other girl." The emotions burst out of Tynise. "And when I told him about the baby, he got all stupid, like ain't no way it could be his."

"I know. Reggie did the same thing. It was ugly," Ruby comforted her.

"It's okay, Tynise." Lauryn joined the hug. "You don't need him. Remember, we got each other."

"Look at that." Ruby lifted her head, pointed to a billboard advertisement for Planned Parenthood and read the caption. "Pregnant and scared? You're not alone."

"Hey, they're talkin' to us," Lauryn said. "Dag, Mari, that girl looks just like you."

"No she don't. Look at how big her belly is. I don't look like that."

"Not now, but you will soon." Ruby pulled out her cell phone.

"Who you callin'?" Lauryn asked

"I'm calling that number. I mean, I know we got the books and everything, but what if there's something we're missing."

The lady on the other side of the phone was sympathetic, full of information, and seemed like she really cared. Ruby grabbed a pen from her backpack and began scribbling down notes. They spent the rest of the afternoon on Marisol's porch planning their trip to Planned Parenthood.

* * *

"Are you sure they gonna see us? We not gonna need our parent's permission or nothing?" Marisol asked Ruby from the front seat of Hector's car.

"For real. Man, I ain't drivin' all the way down there for nothin'," Hector complained.

"No, remember, they told us. You don't need your parent's permission as long as you're over twelve years old."

"And how much is all this gonna cost?" Tynise asked.

"I told you guys. You don't have to pay for anything," Ruby replied. "They hook you up with a lot of stuff. The lady said they have all kinds of programs to help pregnant teens. There's the County Health Department and a bunch of hospitals and churches all over Chicago that hook you up for free. You can get monthly check ups with a doctor and all the prenatal care you need. They give you baby supplies and help you stay in school and get your diploma or GED. Some of them even help you with a ride to your doctor appointments. All they care about is the health of the baby."

"See, I knew it. We all gonna get hooked up. This ain't gonna be nothin'. The man is gonna take care of all the doctor bills and if we all stick together and help each other out, all our babies is gonna come up straight," Lauryn laughed with an I told you so look on her face. Then she took out a blunt to smoke.

"What the hell are you doin'," Tynise screamed at her. "You ain't been smokin' that junk have you?"

"Just a little to settle my stomach, you know. All this mornin' sickness really sucks. I can't even eat right no more. It's just to keep me from pukin'. How am I gonna have a healthy baby if I don't eat right? A little puff every now and then ain't gonna hurt nothin'."

"Lauryn, I swear if you don't throw that junk away right now, I'm gonna slap the taste out your mouth," Tynise threatened.

"God, Lauryn, what's wrong with you?" Ruby added.

"Quit freaking out, damn. I been smokin' for years and it ain't done no harm. What you worried about? It's natural, God given from the earth. It's probably good for the baby. You know Lashanda. She told me she smoked when she was pregnant and her baby turned out fine. Dequan's the most beautiful baby I ever seen."

"Please tell me you don't really believe that," Ruby replied. "You can't actually be that stupid."

"Who you callin' stupid?"

"Throw it out now, Lauryn. I mean it," Tynise barked.

"Okay, already, damn."

Lauryn knew she was outnumbered so there was no use in arguing. She pretended to throw the blunt out the car window, but secretly hid it in her hand.

"Damn, there's a lot of people here," Hector said as they entered the waiting room.

"At least we ain't the only ones," Lauryn commented.

The room was full of teenage girls with a far away look in their eyes, like they were stuck in the middle of a high suspense drama and nervous about the outcome. They stood in the middle of the room not knowing what to do until Ruby noticed a short, Hispanic girl that looked like she was about to deliver at any moment signing in at the front desk.

"Come on, let's sign in," Ruby said.

A heavy set Black woman with thick glasses sat behind a glass barrier. She slid open a small window and handed Ruby a clipboard.

"Sign in please. Your wait will be about an hour or so," she said without looking up from her paperwork.

Each signed in and turned around to find a place to sit. It was standing room only except for two open seats in the corner. Tynise and Lauryn took the seats while Hector and Marisol stood, holding hands, with Ruby standing next to them. They looked around the room dumfounded by a cacophony of screaming babies and anxious expressions on faces whose only worry should be what outfit they were going to where to school the next day.

"Where were you this morning?" Lauryn asked Tynise.

"Just walkin' around. You know it be quiet real early in the morning. I couldn't sleep anyway thinkin' about Tyree."

120

"Forget that fool. He ain't about nothin', that little peanut head, wanna be rapper. You can do better without him."

"I don't know, Lauryn, look at all these girls up in here. They look stressed out, for real. And all these whiny babies, man, it's gonna be hard to do this without Tyree. He had a good job and everything. Why'd he have to be such a dog?"

"They're all dogs, baby. You know that. What made you think that fool was gonna change?"

"I don't know." Tynise paused to think for a moment. "My mom said she was gonna kill me if I didn't stay in school."

"You told her?" Ruby interrupted.

"Yeah, I did. She was pissed. She said I was gonna have to find a way to stay in school and get some kind of job. She said she did it, now I was gonna have to do it, too. Man, this is gonna be hard as hell, but I'm glad we came here." Tyinise picked through a hand full of pamphlets sitting on the table next to her. "Looks like they got a lot of good information here."

"Hey, at least your mother doesn't want you to kill your baby," Ruby sulked.

Tynise looked up at her and said, "She wants you to get an abortion, no way."

"Seriously, she does. I hate that woman. I'm not gonna get any support from her. Reggie called me a hooker, my father will definitely hate me, and my mother wants to kill my baby. I know I'm gonna have to do this on my own."

"It was almost like my mother was expecting it," Lauryn said. "She told me I was gonna have to get a job 'cause she was done raisin' babies. She said she didn't lay down for no baby and she ain't payin' for no baby. So I know I'm on my own. That's okay though, I'll be okay. You're gonna be okay too, Ruby." Lauryn stood up and gave Ruby a hug. "It's okay, your baby will love you no matter what. You're gonna be ten times the mother your mother is, and so will I."

"You think so?"

121

"I know so, Ruby," Marisol said. "Don't worry, you not gonna be alone. We all gonna do this together."

"That's right," Lauryn said. "Look, just 'cause your mother's a loser, don't mean you gonna be one. I know I ain't never gonna leave my baby while I'm out strippin'. Or take my baby to work with me in some sleezy club like my moms did with me."

"So, how you gonna make money," Tynise asked her.

"I can do hair and get paid under the table. Plus, I'm sure there's somethin' in all that stuff to hook us up with some food stamps and free baby gear and stuff," Lauryn replied pointing to the stack of pamphlets and brochures Tynise was still holding in her hands. "Anyway, I know I ain't gonna end up strippin'. Even if I did I wouldn't take my baby to work with me, no way."

"Maybe your mom said that, too, but she didn't have a choice," Tynise said.

"Damn, this is gonna be hard." Ruby had a revelation. "None of us have a job. For real, what are we gonna do?"

"What are you all so worried about," Lauryn said. "Ruby, you already told us how this place was gonna hook us up and after our babies are born we can get food stamps, and you can get cribs real cheap at the mission, free diapers and a lot of junk. Lashanda told me when she had her baby she didn't have to pay for nothin'. They hook you up, for real. I ain't gonna have to be strippin', but if it comes down to it, I'll do what I have to do to feed my baby."

"Damn, girl, you gonna end up strippin', just like your mom." Tynise looked disappointed.

"It is really good money, but I could never do it," Lauryn stood her ground. "I just hate the way the men look at her, you know, like they think they own you over a stinkin' dollar bill. I don't see how my moms did it all these years."

"I know I could never do that," Marisol said.

"Damn right you ain't gonna do that." Hector finally joined the conversation. It took him a little while to shake off the initial shock of being the only man in a room full of pregnant girls.

"Yeah, there's gotta be a better way to make some money without having to take your clothes off. That's just a step away from sellin' it on the streets," Tynise said.

"So, what would you do if your baby was starvin' and you ain't got no money? For real, what you gonna do?" Lauryn challenged Tynise.

"I don't know, but I know I wouldn't be takin' off my clothes for no nasty men," Tynise snapped at her. "I guess I would just work overtime at my job or whatever. I mean we did promise we would help each other out and babysit for each other and stuff, right?"

"That's right," Marisol affirmed. "My family and Hector's family gonna help. They already say so and mi prima got a good crib. She have a baby last year so I'm gonna get a lot of clothes and stuff. We all gonna share. Hector's gonna work part time, after school, and he gonna go college no matter what. And I'm gonna work after school, too. Mi tia thinks she can get me a job at the shop where she makes clothes."

"Damn, girl, you're too smart to be working in some sweat shop," Ruby said with a concerned look on her face. "What about college?"

"No, it's not like that, but it is hard. She works a lot, but I'm gonna be making good money and I'm gonna learn to make good clothes for my baby. You don't know, Ruby. It's easy for you. You family got money. You don't never have to work."

"She's gonna go to college," Hector interrupted. "Right now it's just too much money for me and her to go with the baby coming and everything. It's better for the baby to be with its mother a lot, you know. Then she can go back to school when the baby gets older."

"I know you guys have to make a lot of sacrifices," Ruby replied. "My parents will probably get me a nanny or something. No way they're gonna let me drop out of school. This is gonna be easy. I'll just have my new nanny watch all our babies. Whatever I have, I'm gonna share with you guys. You know you guys are like my sisters. All for one and one for all."

Chapter 20

Over the next month, the girls spent their time comparing symptoms, making plans, and leaning on each other. It was too cold outside to hang out on Marisol's porch or at the park, so Hector dropped them off at Ruby's.

Ruby's seemed like a different world to Marisol, Tynise and Lauryn, too far from their reality to be real or comfortable. Ruby always tried to downplay her money, but that was hard to do in such lavish surroundings.

"Damn, Ruby, your baby's gonna come up like *The Fresh Prince of Bel Air*," Lauryn said as she wandered around the house, her eyes wide open.

"Yeah, I guess that's true, but it's not all about that, you know," Ruby replied.

"No, I don't know what you mean to be honest with you," Tynise said. "I mean, look at this place. I wouldn't worry about nothin' if I lived up in here."

"For real," Lauryn said as they gave each other a high five.

"Just 'cause you got money doesn't mean you don't have problems," Ruby said.

"True that, mo' money, mo' problems," Lauryn sang.

"Yeah, this stuff is cool and expensive and all," Ruby continued, "but it's just stuff. You know what I mean. It's fake.

Everyone up here is all phony. I'd much rather hang out in the hood. At least people down there keep it real."

"Oh, it's real alright," Lauryn laughed.

"Too real for me," Tynise said. "I don't want my baby growin' up around all the bums and gangs down there. I don't care if I don't live around my people. If I had a chance to get outta there, I would in a second. I wanna give my baby everything I never had."

"I feel you," Lauryn agreed.

"It's true, Ruby," Marisol added with a serious look on her face. "Maybe if you was born down there, you not gonna wanna stay down there so much."

"I don't know about you guys, but I'm not throwin' up as much as I used to," Tynise intentionally changed the subject. "I been feelin' pretty good."

"Me, too," Ruby agreed. "It's like I got more energy and everything."

"My boobs is gettin' huge," Lauryn cupped her breasts in her hands. "It's been thirteen weeks. I wonder when I'm gonna start showin'," she said looking at Marisol's protruding belly.

"I can feel my baby growing inside me," Marisol grinned at her stomach, "but I got something funny, look, see this." Marisol pulled up her sweater and tugged down on her jeans to reveal a dark line ascending upwards through the middle of her abdomen. "What is it?"

"I got that too," Tynise jumped up to reveal hers, "and I ain't even showin' that much."

"They didn't tell you about that down at the clinic?" Ruby asked. "They told me I might get a dark line coming up my stomach. They said it happens to women of color. It's normal."

"So, I guess I won't get one," Lauryn said still looking at her belly. But I bet I'm gonna get stretch marks."

"Oh, God, don't remind me," Ruby placed her hand on both sides of her puffy cheeks. "My body's gonna get all jacked up. I'm gonna blow up like a pig." She pinched a bulge of fat growing from her hip, felt a twinge of disgust and lamented over her once perfect

125

body. "I've been getting big all over, except for my belly. At least you got something to show for it."

"Hey, that's just part of it," Lauryn reassured her. "We're all gonna gain weight, but we can get rid of it after the baby is born. Look at my moms. She's had two kids and still looks pretty good for being over thirty. Your mother still got it going on too, Mari."

"Yeah, she still got a nice body and everything. I'm not scared." Marisol smiled.

"Don't sweat it, Ruby." Lauryn pulled a book out of her back pack. "Look what I got."

"Oh, baby names." Marisol perked up. "I know what my name means. Marisol means sea and sun. Mira, in Spanish mar is the sea and sol is the sun, Marisol. It's a sign for life. The sun give life to everything on land and the sea give life to all the animals in the ocean. I think you need to be careful what you gonna name the baby. It gotta be a good, strong name. I love my name."

"Lauryn, remember that girl that named her baby Lil' G. She lived like two floors up from you?" Tynise asked.

"Yeah, I do. Man, that girl was all caught up in the game. Now that boy ain't got no choice but to run with the gangs, you know.

"Uhm, so ghetto," Tynise said and they all laughed.

"What about Hector? What does it mean?" Marisol asked.

"Let's see, Hector," Lauryn thumbed through the book, "Hector means tenacious. Tenacious, what's that?"

"That means he never gives up. It's a strong name for a boy," Ruby answered.

"That's Hector, for real," Marisol said smiling.

"What about Michael? I always liked Michael," Ruby asked.

"Michael means, gift from God. Hey, that's a good one. I'm a use Michael if I have a boy," Lauryn declared.

"Hey, I thought of it first," Ruby argued.

"All I know is I ain't gonna give my baby one of those ghetto names like Sheronda or Laqueasha, or Sheniquea," Tynise said.

"Where do they come up with those names anyway?" Ruby asked.

"Well, Sheniqua comes from she is unique, get it, Sheniqua," Tynise explained. "Sometimes they just blend names together, like my cousin Ronnie and his girlfriend Nikki. They named their baby girl Ronikka. I think it's cute."

"Yeah, like when Quentin and Wanda had their baby. They named her Laquanda. I guess they just threw in the "La" 'cause it sounded good," Lauryn said.

"How you think I got my name?" Tynise asked. "My father's name was Tyrone and my mother's name is Denise, Tynise. That's about the only thing my mother ever told me about him."

"I know one thing," Marisol said with a sour look on her face. "I'm not gonna name my baby after a car like mi prima. She got a baby name Mercedes and one she name Porshia."

"Now that's ghetto," Ruby laughed. "But I think you're right, Mari. A name is important. I want a good strong name for my baby, no matter if it's a girl or a boy. A name should build character. I think it would be cool to have my baby named after a great African king or queen. You know, or some kind of traditional African name to remind him or her about their heritage, like Ashanti or Aaliyah."

"That's a good idea," Lauryn said. "Those old African names is tight, but I wanna find one that ain't been used yet."

"What, you figure you gotta get back with your African roots," Tynise teased Lauryn.

"Shut up, you ain't funny," Lauryn defended herself. "Don't be tryin' me. Did you forget my baby's gonna be half Black? I'm gonna make sure he knows about his African roots and I ain't just talkin' about Martin Luther King. My baby's gonna know where he comes from. I'm gonna have a beautiful, proud mixed baby. You know mixed babies come out lookin' the best anyway. Look at Halle Berry and Mariah Carey."

"That's true, but you got really blonde hair," Tynise reminded her. "That don't mix good with black hair. Your baby's gonna come out with that really curly orange hair and freckles all over his face."

"Whatever. I don't care," Lauryn snapped at her. "I'm gonna love him no matter what. He's still gonna be beautiful to me."

"I know, Lauryn," Tynise replied in a remorseful tone. "I didn't mean nothin'.....Lauryn, are you okay?"

"I don't know. My stomach hurts, like, real bad."

All of a sudden, Lauryn doubled over clutching her stomach and fell to the floor, writhing and groaning. The girls dropped to her side in shock.

"Lauryn, what's wrong," Tynise said stroking her forehead.

"Dios mio, Lauryn, Dios mio." Marisol looked up for help.

Ruby pulled out her cell phone. "I'm calling 911."

* * *

Tynise, Marisol, and Ruby sat quietly in the waiting room. There was nothing any of them could say to ease the tension and suspense. Marisol prayed, Ruby stared out the window thinking about her father, and Tynise was too restless to sit anymore. None of them wanted to think about the possibility that Lauryn could lose her baby. That would mean they could lose their baby too.

"I gotta go for a walk," Tynise said and shuffled away from the waiting area. Her feet barely carried the strength to place one in front of the other. Intuition planted a seed that things were not going well, but she paid it no attention. All she wanted was fresh air.

"That poor girl, there was nothing we could do about the baby." Tynise overheard two nurses talking as she walked to the elevator. One was tall and sturdy while the other was short, lean and walked around in quick, jittery movements.

"You mean the blonde girl. It's a shame, but she did bring it on herself," the short one said with a cynical look on her face.

"How can you be so cold? That child in there is only fifteen years old."

The short nurse stopped moving around and slammed her clipboard on the counter. "Well, she was old enough to smoke marijuana and drink wasn't she. You know how much mess we found in her system and the cigarettes in her purse. She was probably drunk last night. I don't know why these children even bother getting pregnant if they're just going to keep on boozing and drugging. Don't they know they're killing their babies?"

"I know." The tall nurse bowed her head as if she were in prayer. "Maybe we can save the next one."

Tynise ran down the hall to find Lauryn lying motionless in a stale hospital bed. Lauryn turned her head toward Tynise and a tear fell from the corner of her eye on to the pillow.

"You never stopped smoking did you?" Tynise rushed to her bed side with a tone that was more accusing than sympathetic. "How could you do that to your baby?"

"Tynise." Lauryn began to cry uncontrollably, the reality of her actions thrown in her face. "I'm sorry. I'm so stupid. I didn't think. I'm so stupid. God, what'd I do?"

Tynise's heart was softened by the sight of her best friend falling apart. She reached out for Lauryn's hand.

"It's gonna be okay, Lauryn. This is just a bump in the road that's all. We're gonna get over it, just like we always do."

"But I wanted a baby so bad. My baby was like a dream come true to me. You know what I mean."

"I know, but maybe this was supposed to happen. Maybe this is God's way of telling you it's not the right time for you. If it's your dream it will happen some day, just not right now. Your dream is just frozen for a while, that's all."

"Frozen, huh." Lauryn stared off into nowhere for a moment. "I guess we just live in a world of frozen dreams."

"You know you just came up with another name for the hood," Tynise said with a grin.

"What's that?"

"*The Land of Frozen Dreams.*"

129

Chapter 21

"Ain't nobody heard from Lauryn?" Tynise asked Ruby and Marisol. She had to strain her voice to be heard over the commotion in the cafeteria. "I stopped by her place this morning, but she wasn't there again."

"She hasn't been returning any of my phone calls. I hope she's okay all alone in that little apartment. I hope she didn't do anything stupid," Ruby said.

"It's been a month since she lost her baby," Tynise said with a weight of the world written on her face. "She don't call me back either and every time I go by she ain't home."

"She's not gonna pass ninth grade if she keeps missing school. Did she drop out or what?" Ruby asked.

"I don't know, but I think she's okay," Marisol replied. "Lauryn is a tough girl. She just need time to think, that's all."

"I hope you're right. That's one thing about Lauryn, she does know how to take care of herself," Tynise's face relaxed.

"She knows how to take care of herself, alright, but she sure didn't take care of that baby," Ruby said with a sour look on her face.

"I know," Marisol responded with an equally disgusted face. "She didn't have to do all that stuff. She know she gonna hurt the baby."

"She didn't care. I always knew Lauryn could be selfish, but she wasn't thinking about her baby at all," Ruby said. "I get so mad when I think about it."

"You know Lauryn's not a bad person." Tynise felt sorry for her best friend.

"Don't defend her, Tynise. You know what she did was wrong. She had a responsibility to her baby and she just didn't care," Ruby persisted.

"Maybe she just wasn't ready for that responsibility. I'm not sure I am," Tynise admitted.

"I'm not sure either," Ruby continued. "We're all scared, but there's a big difference between being scared and not caring. Babies need a lot of attention. If you don't have the time to care, you shouldn't even have a baby."

* * *

Ruby stood in front of the mirror in her room unable to believe she was five months pregnant. It took her longer to show than the others, so she was especially proud of her hump. She was even proud of the dark line running up the middle of her abdomen. Her reflection had a hypnotizing effect as she stared at her belly, rubbed it with her hands, and hummed a song that almost put her into a trance. She had never felt so close, so at peace, so filled with harmony.

A light tapping on the door interrupted, "Ruby, Ruby, honey, can I come in?"

"Come in Mother," Ruby answered, annoyed at the disruption.

"I'm sorry to bother you, but I have great news," she said with a broad smile. "Your father's coming home tomorrow. I don't know how long he's going to be able to stay, but he's coming home. He's coming home, honey. Isn't that great news?"

A shockwave of uncertainty hit Ruby. She looked down and gently stroked her bare belly. "Does he know?"

"I had to tell him, Ruby. He is your father."

"What did he say?"

"He's disappointed, of course, but he loves you, honey. He just wants the best for you. We'll all sit down and talk when he gets here. Oh, I have so much to do before tomorrow."

Ruby's mother rushed out the door leaving her to wallow in anxiety. Her hands began to shake at the thought of her father's judgment bearing down on her like a lion on a gazelle in the open plain. She had to pick up the phone and reach out.

"Mari?"

"Hey, Ruby."

"Mari, thank God you're home. I had to talk to somebody."

"What's wrong?"

"You're not gonna believe it. God, this sucks. He's gonna ruin everything."

"What, Ruby, what?"

"My father's coming home."

"Really, when?"

"Tomorrow."

"No way."

"Yes, he is, tomorrow. I don't know what to do."

"Does he know about the baby?"

"He knows and I bet he and my mother are already making plans. They're gonna gang up on me. I know it. What am I gonna do?"

"Ruby, they can't make you get rid of the baby. They not gonna force you. You gonna have a good baby and then they gonna see what a good mama you can be."

"You don't know my father, Mari. It's his way or the highway. Trust me, he's not gonna see anything he doesn't wanna see. I'm gonna have to figure something out."

"It's your father. Don't worry, he gonna understand."

"You don't understand. My family doesn't work like yours. He's not gonna understand. God, this is gonna be so much harder now that he's back."

"I'm sorry, Ruby. I don't know what to say. If things get real bad, you can stay here. Remember, we gonna stick together, no matter what."

"Thank you. I'll be okay, I guess."

Ruby hung up the phone more filled with worry than before she called. She wished her father were more like Marisol's, caring and understanding. But that was not her reality. Getting pregnant at fifteen was not part of the lieutenant colonel's plan. It was fun to think about how much the pregnancy would piss him off when he was on the other side of the world, but he was coming home.

She spent the night tossing and turning, anticipating the lieutenant colonel's criticism, his rejection and his disappointing glare that spawned her rebellion. His flight was coming early in the morning so she only had a few more hours to enjoy the peaceful silence of the house. Just as she was falling into a light sleep, a familiar, commanding voice bellowing in the hallway broke her respite.

"I don't care if she's sleeping. Wake her up. I want to talk to that young lady right now."

The butterflies exploded in Ruby's stomach and her hands started shaking as she heard the foot steps approaching in those heavy boots he wore.

"Rise and shine, young lady. It's zero six hundred." The voice echoed down the hallway.

She pretended to be asleep, then, realized his unrelenting nature would never let her rest. She begrudgingly lifted her head, eased out of bed and put a robe over the panties and t-shirt she slept in. A solid knock swung the door open and was standing face to face with the lieutenant colonel. He looked as tall and strong as she remembered. His physique was muscular and sturdy, molded by hours of training and the rigorous exercise that came with military life. Her eyes fixated on the pulsating vein she remembered bulged from his forehead whenever he was mad. The lieutenant colonel was never one for hugs and kisses, so Ruby wasn't expecting a warm, fuzzy reunion. Still, she was not prepared for what came out of his mouth.

133

Mark Miller

"How could you let this happen to yourself?" the lieutenant colonel barked, his eyes fixed on the developing bulge sticking out from her robe. "You're not keeping that baby. You'll have to give it up. You're way too young to raise a child and your mother and I are not raising any more kids. How could you be so stupid? Ruby, you have disappointed me more now than you ever have before."

"God, you're just like her," Ruby yelled back, pointing at her mother. "You're not gonna kill my baby."

"We're not talking about an abortion, Ruby. It's too late for that. We want to give it up for adoption. It would be better that way," Ruby's mother said with a pleading look on her face. "There are so many good, reputable adoption agencies that can help. We could make sure it goes to a happy home."

"I won't give up my baby," Ruby shrieked. "You can't make me do that. I know I have rights. You can't make me give up my baby."

"What the hell makes you think you can tell me what I can and can't do in my own home," the lieutenant colonel snapped at her. "I hope you don't plan on raising that baby in this house."

Ruby stood speechless, frozen and shocked by his reaction.

"What are you going to do?" the lieutenant colonel barked on. "You moving out, dropping out of school, getting a job? Have you even thought about how much money you have to make to raise a child on your own? And what about college? You can't even take care of yourself. How are you going to raise a child, work and go to school at the same time? You really didn't think this one through, did you?"

"Don't worry about it. My friends will help me. I don't need you." Ruby tried to walk past him, but he grabbed her by the arm.

"Greg, no," Ruby's mother shouted.

He was strong but Ruby was mad. She quickly snatched her arm away and ran through the door. The lieutenant colonel caught up with her just as she began her descent down the stairs and grabbed her from behind. He spun her around with one jerk of his powerful arm and began shaking her by the shoulders.

"Who the hell do you think you're running away from?" He yelled at her. His face so close she could feel the spray of his words and the throbbing of the vein on his forehead. "You're going to stand at attention and listen, young lady. I'm your father."

"No, Greg, please." Ruby's mother tried to hold him back, but her effort was abruptly met by the back off his hand. The slap cracked across her face like booming thunder and she flew back down the hallway.

The distraction gave Ruby just enough time to attempt another escape, but the lieutenant colonel still had one hand firmly gripping her arm. She had never felt so defenseless. The sight of her mother lying helpless on the floor sent her into hysteria. "Get off me, get off," she yelled, slapping at him with her free arm.

"Stop it, Ruby, shut up."

"Get off me."

Stuck in a stalemate, Ruby and the lieutenant colonel pushed and pulled at one another. Somehow Ruby broke free, but she slipped and her momentum carried her down a steep flight of hard wood stairs.

"You monster, what did you do?" Ruby's mother recovered and stood at the top of the stairs staring down on Ruby's motionless body. "Call 911, call 911," she mumbled to herself as she fumbled around for the phone.

Mark Miller

Chapter 22

"We're expecting a full recovery for your daughter," a short, balding, doctor with thick, glasses told Ruby's parents in a matter of fact tone, "but she lost the baby. She took a pretty bad fall, but beside some deep tissue bruises, she's going to be fine. We want to keep her overnight to monitor for internal trauma, but I don't forsee any complications and she will be able to have children in the future."

"Oh, thank God," Ruby's mother sighed in relief.

"The most important thing is that Ruby's okay. Everything turned out for the best." The lieutenant colonel said with a pleased look on his face.

"How did it happen?" The doctor looked curiously at the lieutenant colonel.

"She fell down the stairs. She's always been clumsy, right honey." The lieutenant colonel turned to his wife for support, but she did not reply. Instead, she lowered her eyes to the ground in an attempt to hide the anger and shame on her face.

The doctor reached out, mistaking her shame for pain, and placed a sympathetic hand on her shoulder. "I am sorry for your loss, but take solace in the fact that your daughter is healthy, young and still has the rest of her life ahead of her."

Ruby lay in her hospital bed staring at the walls thinking of ways to hate the lieutenant colonel. Her baby was gone and it was his fault.

"Ruby." Her mother tapped lightly on the door before entering. "Ruby, honey, I'm so sorry. I tried to stop him. I'm so sorry about the baby," she said in a voice that begged for forgiveness.

Ruby whipped her head toward the door and pushed her words through clenched teeth. "Liar. Don't come near me. You know you wanted it gone. You never cared about my baby. Leave me alone."

"Ruby, please, you know your father didn't mean it. He has a temper, but he didn't do it on purpose. He can be cruel, but he's not a monster."

"Whatever. Why are you defending that baby killer?"

"Ruby, listen, I didn't mean for you to fall." The lieutenant colonel slid into the room behind his wife. "It was an accident. You were there. You slipped and fell down the stairs. I'm just glad you're safe. You'll see. Everything turned out for the best."

"For the best," Ruby screamed. "Are you sick? You wanted my baby gone and you made it happen. Baby Killer. You always get what you want, right, sir." She raised her hand to her brow, threw an indignant salute then let her body fall back unto the bed. "God, I can't believe this," she cried in her pillow. "You're trying to blame it on me. Get out of here. God, please, just leave me alone."

"Come on Greg, she's not ready to talk to you. Give it some time." She led her husband out the room and turned to Ruby. "I love you, honey. I'll be back to check on you later."

"Whatever," Ruby mumbled under her breath.

She flipped through the TV for the rest of the afternoon. Tyra Banks, Jerry Springer and Judge Judy provided perfect zone out material. But it only worked for a while. She couldn't shake the feel of her unborn child or resist the need to close her eyes and imagine what it would have looked like. But her mind's eye could only conjure faceless babies.

Just as she was sinking into a deep depression Tynise and Marisol knocked on the door and ran straight to her bedside.

"Oh, Ruby, I'm so sorry," Marisol said, stroking her hand.

"It's gonna be okay, Ruby." Tynise held her other hand from the other side of the bed.

"It's not okay. That bastard killed my baby. He wanted it gone ad he made it happen. I hate him."

"Who, Ruby, what happen?" Marisol asked.

"My father. He pushed me down the stairs. He killed my baby."

"No, Dios mio, no."

"He was shaking me and screaming. I'll never forget the look in his eyes, like they were on fire. Then he pushed me. He said it was an accident, but he pushed me. I know it. He hated my baby. He wanted it dead."

"Oh my God," Tynise gasped. You gotta tell somebody. You gotta tell the police. You can't let him get away with that."

"You don't understand, Tynise. My father is like a war hero to people around here. He'll just get some high powered lawyer. I can't really prove anything. He's just gonna say it was an accident. There's no way I can win."

"What about your mother?" Marisol asked. "Will she help you?"

"I don't think so. She waned to get rid of my baby, too. I don't know. He did smack the taste out her mouth before he pushed me down the stairs." Ruby paused to think. "I wonder how long he's been smacking her around?"

"He hit her, too?" Tynise asked. "You should talk to her Ruby. She might help you. She might be tired of gettin' hit."

"I don't know. I don't know what to do."

"I think you have to tell somebody," Tynise advised. "Why don't you tell your doctor the next time you see him. If you tell him it was abuse, he has to do somethin' about it."

"That's right," Marisol agreed. "You got to do something. Come on, Ruby, I never see you give up on nothing."

"They would have to open an investigation," Ruby thought to herself out loud. "I wonder what the crowd at the country club and the brass at the army will think when they find out he's being investigated for pushing his pregnant daughter down the stairs. The scandal alone would crush their little world."

The plan allowed Ruby to smile for the first time since "the accident".

Marisol and Tynise stayed for a couple more hours planning the demise of the lieutenant colonel and laughing at the losers on daytime TV. Ruby felt better by the time they left. She had a solid plan for revenge. A plan that made her feel in control and that eased the pain, a little.

Ruby woke up the next morning feeling numb all over. She had gone through the ritual of brushing her teeth and combing her hair. She sat on the bed staring blankly at the wall, waiting for her mother to come pick her up.

"Ruby." A meek voice whispered, but Ruby hardly noticed it. "Ruby, it's me, over here."

The voice pestered Ruby until she slowly turned her head. "Lauryn, oh my God, where have you been?"

"I've been around, you know, doin' my thing," Lauryn responded in an upbeat voice.

Ruby's expression turned sour at the sight of Lauryn in high heels, jeans, and way too much make up. She had the haggard look of one of the girls that stand on the street corner, over worked and tired.

"I'm so sorry about your baby, Ruby. I know how you feel. You know, most times when I say that, I don't really mean it. But this time I really, really do know how you feel."

"I know you do, Lauryn, thank you. How are you doing? I mean, do you get over it?"

"No, I don't think so," Lauryn answered with her head bowed.

They sat together in silence, side by side on the bed. Ruby tried not to, but couldn't help notice Lauryn's worn, chipped nails and gnarled hands. They were wrinkled and twisted, like the hands of someone twice her age.

"Where have you been, Lauryn? Nobody's seen, you in weeks?"

139

"I told you. Just doin' my thing, you know," Lauryn answered with a smile, but her eyes were crying.

"Doing what thing? What you been up to? You don't look so good."

"I been workin' as a waitress down at Clancy's."

"That old hole in the wall where they play pool?"

"Yeah, it ain't that bad. It ain't nothin' but the same busters from around the way, they just old now, that's all. They be hanging out, playing pool, and junk. You know, they be fightin' sometimes, but it ain't no big thing."

"You should go back to school."

"Please, you know I ain't never been nothin' in school. I'm doin' okay, but I didn't come here to talk about me. I came here to see how you was doin'."

"I don't know how I'm doing. I don't know if I feel anything. How did you hear about what happened to me, anyway? Have you talked to Mari or Tynise?"

"No, but I guess I should. I just heard it. You know you can't keep nothin' down around here. I know you ain't from the hood, but you a part of it now."

"So, all my business is in the streets." Ruby looked upset for a moment then a dull expression changed her face. "It doesn't matter though. It really doesn't."

"I know it don't. People is gonna talk. You know that. Ruby, when I lost my baby, I thought I was gonna die. I didn't wanna deal with nothin' or nobody, but then it hit me. I'm still young and a lot of girls miscarry their first time. I can still have baby and you can, too."

"I don't know, Lauryn. I still can't believe my baby is gone. I didn't even have a name for him yet, or her. It could have been a girl. I don't even know. I wanted it to be a surprise. Why didn't I ever find out? What about yours? Was it a girl or a boy?"

"I don't know. I guess I wanted it to be a surprise, too. I'm definitely gonna find out early next time."

140

"Next time?" Ruby paused to think. "I don't know about next time."

Chapter 23

"Did you hear from Ruby?" Marisol asked Tynise over lunch in the cafeteria.

They had been spending almost all their free time together lately. As the last surviving members of Baby Club, they felt a kindred need to keep each other company, like nothing would happen to their babies if they were together.

"No, not yet. I can't believe she'd just drop outta school. First Lauryn then Ruby. I know Lauryn still stays at her place. Her mother said she was still there."

"Did she tell you where she is?"

"No. I told her Lauryn ain't been comin' to school but she don't care."

"Tynise, what if something happen to my baby," Marisol said, looking down and rubbing her belly. "I don't think I can take it."

"Don't think like that. That's not gonna happen to us. Lauryn lost her baby 'cause she was druggin' and drinkin' and Ruby's father killed her baby. None of that's gonna happen to us. We take care of our babies."

"God, I can't believe I'm almost seven months," Marisol said. "I still not even showing that much."

"I know. Don't say it. I know I'm gettin' big as a house."

"You supposed to be big. That means you got a healthy baby. Dios mio, I think there's something wrong with my baby."

"Mari, stop it. Didn't your doctor say the baby was healthy at your last visit?"

"Yeah."

"Then quit trippin'. Didn't she say your weight was normal? Every girl gains weight different, right."

"I guess." Marisol smiled and appreciated the kind words but continued to worry. "I bet it's gonna hurt when the baby come out."

"You had to bring that up."

"Mi tia, Sonya, says she was in labor por viente horas with her baby. She says it was like a thousand donkeys was kicking in her stomach. And when the baby come, she say it was like giving birth to a watermelon, everything stretching and ripping. Aye, I'm so scared."

"I know. My mom said there's no pain like it in the whole world. She said she was in labor for nine hours with me, but it was much worse with Quincy. He was a breech baby. You know, when they come out butt first. I think that's what they call it. Anyway, she was in labor for eighteen hours with him and he still wouldn't come out right. They had to give her a c-section."

"You mean when they cut open your belly and take the baby that way?"

"Yep, it's like surgery. They cut your stomach open and take the baby out." Tynise's face turned squeamish. "You should see her scar."

"Aye, so many things can happen. I'm really scared now."

"I know. If regular child birth is so painful, I bet a c-section hurts like hell."

"But Quincy came out okay, didn't he?"

"He came out fine, but my mom said she was sore for weeks."

"I'm not so scared about the pain. I just don't want nothing to happen to my baby. I can't wait to be a mama to my little girl. I'm gonna teach her to cook and make clothes, all the things my mama teach me. Oh, I can't wait. We gonna have so much love for each other."

"You know you gonna have a girl? The doctor told you?"

"Si. At first I didn't wanna know, but Hector's mama wanna know so she could get the room ready for the baby. She gonna have her own room over there."

"You're gonna stay with Hector's parents?"

"Yeah, they want us to stay there. They say they have more room over there and they want to make sure Hector don't forget about his school and all."

"I'm gonna have a boy," Tynise said with trepidation in her voice.

"Oh, Tynise, I'm so happy for you. Hector really wanted a boy, too, but he gonna love his baby girl just the same."

"You so lucky. You got everythin' worked out. Your baby's gonna have a nice house with her own room, you got two sets of grandparents to help you baby sit, and you still got Hector. Everything's perfect for you." Tynise paused for a moment. "I don't know why I thought Tyree would be there for me."

"We gonna be there for you Ruby. My family will help you with the babysitting and stuff. It will be okay."

"I don't know. It's not gonna be the same without Lauryn, you know. This was all her idea and now she's not even around. That's messed up."

"I know. I miss her, too."

Neither said a word as they sat, staring down at their food, thinking about where Lauryn and Ruby might be. After a few moments, Tynise broke the silence. "My mom thinks I should give my baby up for adoption. I don't want to, but it's gonna be so hard. I don't know. I thought it was gonna be cool with all four of us helpin' each other out and everythin', but without Lauryn and Ruby, I don't know. You got your family, but my mom works all the time. She already said she ain't gonna help me watch the baby."

"You not gonna give away the baby? Please, don't think like that. We gonna help you. It's gonna be okay."

"I don't know. It's just not gonna be the same."

"Just think, Tynise. You always gonna have your baby, no matter what. That's the most important thing. You can't give that up."

"Your parents ain't gonna be able to watch my baby all the time."

"Por que no? They gonna be taking care of my baby. They can watch your baby too. Mama loves you."

"I don't know. Maybe sometimes, but all the time when I'm at school or work or whatever, that's askin' a lot."

"It's gonna be okay. You worry too much."

Tynise didn't respond. How could Marisol understand? It was all good for her. Her cheerful disposition gnawed at Tynise's nerves. "Where do you think Ruby is?" she asked in a blatant attempt to escape the waves of optimism.

"I don't know. I pray for her every night."

"I'm afraid for her, you know, the way her father killed her baby. That abusive son of a bitch. He better not be beatin' up on her. We should call the police on him or somethin'. There ain't no way he's gonna get away with killin' Ruby's baby."

"I know. I want to kill him too."

"I bet if we called the police, he's just gonna get some high price lawyer. It's like Ruby said. It's his word against ours and he's, like, a war hero. Man, it's gonna be hard to prove anything."

"Maybe if we go over there to spend the night and put some poison in his food or something," Marisol suggested with a grin on her face.

"That's not a bad idea."

"Or maybe we could get some bangers to jump him on his way to work. Hector knows a few cholos."

"Now you talkin', Mari, or some crackheads. Them fools do anything for a little bit of money. That'd show that bastard, for real."

The thought of sweet revenge had the two laughing so hard they hardly noticed the zoo like raucous of the other kids throwing bits of food and paper, yelling profanity, and rhythmically pounding beats on the cafeteria tables.

All of a sudden their light moment was interrupted by two cholos standing in front of them obviously joking with one another. They were typical Mexican gang bangers wearing the typical cholo gear; a wife beater t-shirt covered by a short sleeve, plaid shirt, bandanas that concealed greasy, jet black hair and pants that sagged half way down their back sides.

"Hey, don't you hang with that snow bunny," one of them asked Tynise with a silly grin on his face. What's her name?"

"I don't know, man, but I think she was callin' herself Snowflake. Did you know she was shakin' that thing down at Teasers?" The other one added as his hips gyrated back and forth.

"What the hell you fools talkin' about?" Tynise barked at them.

"We saw your girl, gettin' buck naked at the strip club Friday night. I know it was her. Ain't too many rubias 'round here."

"You saw Lauryn dancin' at the strip club?" Tynised screeched. "You sure it was her?"

"Yeah, man, it was her. The one that be hangin' with you guys all the time. But her name ain't Lauryn no more, it's Snowflake. Ad you can't call what she was doin' dancin', more like humpin'. What you think, man."

"Hey, I ain't mad at it. I'm just lookin' for a private dance," the other one said, still grinning and gyrating. "She was bouncin' with it, rollin' with it, droppin' it hot, workin' that pole. You know I'm gonna smash that, for real."

"Shut up, fool. Get outta here," Tynise yelled at them as they faded off into the crowd.

"That can't be true, can it, Tynise?" Marisol asked.

"I hope not, but I wouldn't put it past Lauryn to do somethin' like that. She's had a hard time comin' up. Sometimes she don't think a lot before she do stuff. What was the name of that club?" Tynise asked herself out loud. "Teasers, wasn't it?"

Chapter 24

Tynise couldn't get Lauryn off her mind, knowing what she was doing. She didn't want to believe it, but she knew the cholos had no reason to lie. She also knew Lauryn well enough to know stripping was an option for her. Tynise never understood how women could take off their clothes for a bunch of slobbering, drunk men. Her mother had worked hard, double shifts and two jobs when it was hard to make ends meet, but she never had to strip. Nevertheless, she knew Lauryn understood it. She remembered the conversations they had about the money her mother brought home from stripping. Lauryn always made fun of her for giving it all away to booze or drugs or whatever guy was slapping her around at the time, but she admired her mother for being able to "bring home the bacon". She bragged that if she had that much money she would never let some man take it away form her. She never saw her mother as being wrong for what she did, just weak for not being able to handle her business.

Tynise knew she wouldn't be able to rest until she saw Lauryn so she decided to track her down after school. Marisol wanted to go, too, but Hector was taking her to a doctor appointment. It didn't take long for Tynise to find Teasers. She simply asked a couple of boys hanging out on the corner. Growing up in the projects had toned her intuition and gave her good instincts for who she could and couldn't talk to on the streets. She stayed away from the zombie like junkies, always scratching, twitching, snorting, shooting up or begging for change. They were harmless, especially when they realized she didn't have any money. The whore beating pimps left her alone. They sensed the weak, vulnerable ones, open to their game. Tynise was not on their radar, but she knew to keep her distance. Although she had seen the gang bangers beat down rivals, stab and shot one another, she had no fear of them. They were the same little boys she had known all her life, all grown up with guns. The bangers knew everyone and everything in the hood.

Tynise had hoped Lauryn was at least dancing at a nice place She imagined Teasers was one of those swank spots uptown where the business men in suits went to spend their money, but she knew it was in the part of town where only bangers, users, and people who had nothing to lose frequented.

Besides a couple of winos slumping over their brown bags, the street was empty. Tynise didn't know if Lauryn would be there or if the club would be open at four in the afternoon, but the red, neon light was flashing, except for the "a" and the second "e", so she figured it was open. She pushed on a heavy, squeaky door to find a dark hallway lit by a single red light bulb protruding from the wall. She cautiously walked down the hallway with both eyes wide open and stopped at a pedestal at the end of the corridor. She thought it was a logical place to pay a cover charge, but there was no one there to take any money or check for I.D. She found the courage to push her way through the thick, red, velvet curtains leading to the bar and stretched her head around the corner to sneak a peek. She had never been in a strip club before and although she was experiencing mixed emotions; her curiosity far outweighed her apprehension.

The room was so dark it was hard to make out faces, just the silhouettes of a heavy set woman cleaning glasses behind the bar, a tall skinny woman dancing by herself in a corner, and a short, stocky woman giving a lap dance behind a transparent partition. It reminded her of the strip clubs in the movies, dark and sleazy with strings of small red lights lining the stage and poles. Tynise squinted her eyes

148

and tried to find Lauryn through the smoky haze, but she couldn't see her anywhere.

"Welcome to Teasers," a deep voice called out from nowhere. "Coming to the stage is a new addition to our little family. Welcome Snowflake and remember lets keep those tips coming."

Tynise wondered who he was asking to tip. There were only two customers in the whole place, the guy getting a lap dance and an old guy at the bar playing a video poker game. Tynise backed herself into a corner and closed her eyes for a moment. She knew what was coming, but she wasn't ready to see her best friend that way.

Lauryn emerged from behind a black curtain and stumbled on to the stage wearing a strategically ripped t-shirt that read "hot stuff" in big red letters, a red thong, and matching red pumps with stiletto heels. She looked oblivious to her surroundings as she swayed to a slow, rhythmic song with a heavy hip-hop beat. The old man at the video game turned around for a look, but didn't leave his seat. As soon as his lap dance was over, the other guy sat down next to the stage and put up a single dollar bill as bait. Lauryn sauntered her way to him, smiling and writhing. Tynise stood with her mouth agape shocked to see what her best friend would do for a single dollar bill.

She *danced* two songs, placed the two single dollar bills in her thong and rushed off the stage to sit next to the guy that tipped her. Tynise watched her work the guy like a pro, like she'd been doing it for years. And she felt Lauryn's shame when the guy wouldn't even buy her a drink. Tynise guessed that he had already spent all his money on the lap dance. By the time the tall skinny girl took the stage for her turn, the old man at the video game had already left. Lauryn took his place at the game. Tynise couldn't tell if she was playing or just staring into the screen.

Pity, sympathy, frustration, and a hundred other emotions ran through Tynise like the flow of raging rapids, but anger was the most persistent of them all. She stormed over to Lauryn to let out the rage.

"What the hell are you doin' here?" Tynise barked as she grabbed Lauryn by the arm.

"Hey, Ty, what's up girl?" Lauryn spun around on her stool, jumped up, and gave Tynise a big hug.

"Oh, God, no," Tynise sighed.

She only had to take one look into Lauryn's glassy eyes to realize she was wasted in a way she had never seen her before. Not just stoned on a blunt or drunk, she had the same quivering pupils and jittery movements as the crack addicts who roamed the streets of her neighborhood.

"Lauryn, what you doin'? You don't have to do this. This is beneath you."

"Beneath me," she laughed. "What am I, the Queen of England?"

"It's not funny. What happened to doin' hair?"

"I gotta wait 'til a seat opens up at all the places 'round here and it takes money to open your own place. It don't matter. This is easy money right here. All I gotta do is shake it a little and I get paid."

"Yeah, I see how much you get paid. How far you think two dollars a dance is gonna get you."

"This is just the slow time. It really picks up at night amd on the weekends. I made two hundred bucks last Friday and that's all in one night. I just have to work days for a while 'cause I'm new, but after I'm here a while, I'll be workin' nights and gettin' paid."

"Is this really how you wanna get paid? And what the hell are you on?"

"Quit trippin', Ty, damn. It's just a little somethin' to take off the edge."

The look in Lauryn's eyes reminded Tynise of her crack addicted cousin, Lateesha, who stayed with them a couple of years ago. No matter how hard Tynise's mother tried to help her, she always disappointed them.

"I don't know what to say to you, Lauryn. Please, don't do this. You don't have to do this. Please, let me help you."

"I don't need no help." Lauryn's demeanor changed and she snapped at Tynise. "I know what I'm doin'. You be comin' up in

150

here trippin' and talkin' junk. What's up with that? You need to quit trippin'. Just leave me alone."

At that moment, Tynise realized there was nothing more she could say. One of her biggest fears had been realized. Lauryn had become her mother and there was nothing she could do to stop it.

"I'm gonna pray for you, Lauryn. I want you to come see me when you get ready to talk." Tynise threw her arms around Lauryn, gave her a big hug and walked away.

"Where you goin', Ty? Come on, you know I be playin'. Come on, where you goin'?"

It was hard for Tynise to ignore the pleas, but she knew, at this point, there was nothing else she could do. She rushed to the phone when she got home to call Marisol, but all she got was the answering machine. There was only one other person she could possibly talk to about this so she sat, staring out the window, waiting for her mother to get home from work.

"Mom," Tynise waited for Jasmine to go to bed before she brought up the subject, "I need to talk to you about something."

"Yes, go ahead, baby. I like to think you can talk to me about anything."

"I'm worried about Lauryn. She ain't been at school in weeks and she started strippin' at the club. But worst of all, I think she's using some hard drugs, you know, like Lateesha."

"Oh, Lord, Jesus, please save that child," Tynise's mother called out and threw her hands up to the sky.

"I know, mama, Lauryn's my best friend. I wanna help her, but she just wasn't hearing it. What can I do?"

"Well, baby, I don't think there is much you can do until she's ready to hear you. I hope you learned that from Lateesha."

"I know. I did."

"It's no surprise, the way her mother is. That poor child never had a chance. I tried to show her a different way. That's why I let her stay here so much, but I always knew it was going to be hard for her. That girl is so free spirited. No matter what I tried to tell her, you know that girl is going to do whatever she wants to. That's the problem with you kids trying to grow up so quick. You don't want to listen to nobody."

"She was doin' okay until she lost her baby. I never seen her so happy."

"Tynise," she reached across the kitchen table and held her daughter's hands tightly, "have you given any thought to giving your baby up for adoption, like we talked about?"

"A little, I don't know. There's so much goin' on. I can't think about that right now."

"Well, you should think about it, baby. You have no idea how hard having this baby is going to make things for you. Lord knows I love my babies and I don't believe in no regrets, but I sure would have waited to have my babies if I had a chance to do it all over again. I had so many plans. I was going to go to nursing school and be a R.N., but once I got pregnant. Well, let's just say the time really slips away from you. I've been working to pay the bills and keep you and your brother and sister fed ever since."

"I know it's been hard for you, mama, but we'll get by. At least my baby will be here for me."

"That's my point, Tynise. You know how hard it's been for me. Your baby may be there for you, but how you gonna be there for it? How on earth are you going to finish school, get a job, and raise a baby? You're going to have to do all that and more. You know I ain't got no extra money to help you. We're barely getting by as it is. You're going to have to get a job, there's just no way around that. Baby, ain't saying you can't do it. I'm just saying it's going to be very hard on you. You have the rest of your life to start a family. Get yourself a good education and build a good foundation for yourself first. Then you can find a good man, one that can meet you at your own level. This just ain't the right time for you to have a baby. I haven't been working all these years for you to end up like me."

"I know, Mom, but has your life really been so bad?"

"Don't get me wrong. I love my babies. You know that, but I did make it very hard on myself."

"I don't know. It would be so hard to give my baby away. I mean, how would you feel if you had given away me or Jasmine or Quincy? I don't know if I could ever forgive myself."

"I know, baby. It would be the hardest decision you ever have to make. I know it sounds selfish, but it's your life. You only get one shot at it. I did the best I could, but it's not like you were born with a lot of advantages. You're already going to have to work hard for everything you get. Why make it harder on yourself?"

"I don't know, Mom. I don't know," Tynise said as the two sat at the kitchen table holding each others hands. "I guess I have a lot to think about. Thanks for the advice. I love you."

"I love you too baby."

Chapter 25

Over the next two months, Tynise and Marisol thought a lot about Lauryn and Ruby, but they were too concerned with their own bodies to do anything but pray for their lost friends. They were both due any day now and it had been especially uncomfortable for them due to June temperatures in the nineties and humidity that could choke a camel.

Usually, Tynise had no problem sleeping, but the baby had been kicking especially hard and she couldn't find a comfortable spot. She pulled herself out of bed at 5a.m. and stood naked in front of her mirror looking at her body, feeling her baby squirm. Across town Marisol was also having trouble sleeping. Her stomach was cramping, not hard, but it felt different than the usual baby kicking. There was a combination of pressure and pain. She stood in front of the mirror in her room wondering about the changes delivery would put her body through.

Her belly had grown, but she had not gained much weight elsewhere. She stroked her belly with pride and admired her curves and buldges. She wore the stretch marks lining her stomach and hips as a badge of honor, a free pass to the sisterhood of women. Now, she would finally have something to contribute to those conversations when her mother and aunts sat around trading horror stories about the agony of their childbirths.

Tynise wasn't as comfortable with the condition of her body. She had gained a lot of weight, not just in her stomach, but in her legs, hips, arms, and face. She had always felt her face was too round, her hips were too wide, and her breasts were too big for her four foot, eleven inch frame. But, now, as she stood in front of the mirror, all she saw was big. The stretch marks surrounding her stomach and breasts were the last straw. She knew it would be hard enough to loose the extra weight, but the stretch marks would stay with her forever.

For the first time, Tynise thought of her baby as a mistake. Her mother's warnings haunted her thoughts, bringing waves of uncertainty. *How am I ever gonna lose this weight? Am I gonna be able to earn enough money to raise my baby right? What kind of job am I gonna be able to get? Will I have to drop out of school? God, I'm gonna end up strippin' like Lauryn just to feed my baby. What if I don't have a choice? Mom don't have no money to help me. I'm never gonna be able to save enough money for college. I always wanted to go to college. God, this is gonna be so hard. Maybe Mom was right. I wonder how much they pay if I give it up for adoption? Could I get enough money for college? Am I ever gonna get rid of these stretch marks?*

While Tynise gazed into the mirror, imagining the rest of her best years fade away, Marisol gazed with pride at the beginning of a new phase in her life. She smiled from ear to ear as she stroked her stomach and formed a mental image of herself, Hector and their five future children sitting around the dinner table enjoying a big pot of pozole.

All of a sudden, Marisol felt a wet sensation around her inner thighs. At first she thought it was one of those little spurts of pee that came out sometimes when she coughed, sneezed or laughed. She had accepted them as just another one of those annoying things that came with being pregnant, like the throwing up, the stretch marks, and the crazy mood swings. But this time, when she went to wipe, it felt different. The liquid was thick and so clear it shocked her into running down the hall. "Mama, Mama, look. I think my water is breaking," she said trembling in front of her mother, her legs still wet with the slime.

"Aye, mi hija, it's okay. Don't worry, it's supposed to happen like that. Just relax. Come on, I'm gonna get the bag and we gonna go to the hospital right now, okay."

"Mama, I'm scared." Marisol clutched her belly and looked into her mother's eyes with the innocence of a lost puppy.

"I know, hija, I know, don't worry. I'm gonna be with you the whole time."

Marisol, her mother and father, twin brothers, sister and cousin all piled into the family mini van. They sped through traffic beeping the horn and yelling out the window. Fortunately, the hospital was only a few miles away. They made such a raucous storming through the lobby the nursing staff gave Marisol their undivided attention. Marisol's parents, overflowing with anticipation over the birth of their first grandchild, made sure everything was planned in advance. They had called the hospital before they left and by the time Hector and his parents arrived, Marisol was in her room and her doctor was on the way.

Both prospective grandfathers paced in the waiting area while Hector's mother watched Marisol's sister, twin brothers and cousin. Only Hector and Marisol's mother were allowed in the delivery room.

"Don't worry, mi hija, you got a good doctor. Everything's gonna be okay," Marisol's mother said in a soothing voice as she stroked her daughter's hair. She and Hector took their places on opposite sides of the bed and held her hands through the entire delivery. Hector couldn't bear to witness the sight of the baby's head pushing through his fun zone, so he spent the entire time staring into Marisol's eyes and offering words of encouragement. He was Marisol's cheerleader now.

Although the contractions were mild at first, they were a new, strange experience to Marisol. She wasn't accustomed to her insides twisting and churning. It was more uncomfortable than painful, but, overall, not knowing what to expect was the hardest part.

"Try to relax and use these small contractions to adjust your body for child birth. You have some time before the strong contractions begin. You're doing great," the doctor said in a nonchalant manner as he eased his way toward the door.

"Aye, Mama, it don't feel right." Marisol grew more nervous with every little contraction and wondered how she would be able to handle the big ones.

"Hey, where you going? She said it don't feel right. You gotta do somethin'," Hector yelled at the doctor before he was able to make his escape.

"Hector," Marisol's mother interrupted, "he's not supposed to do nothing right now. Marisol is gonna have some pain. It's okay. She's gonna be okay." She nodded at the doctor. He nodded back and left the room.

The rest of the family waited and prayed for good news. All of them would have stayed until the baby came, but the twins were bugging the nursing staff so much Hector's mother had to take them home and put them to bed. They were good for the first three hours, but there was only so much you could do to entertain two rambunctious six year old boys in a quiet hospital waiting room. Marisol's sister and cousin left with them. It was their job to make sure everything was ready for the baby's arrival.

The contractions grew stronger as the hours passed and although she was in pain, Marisol felt good, safe and secure. The doctor, on the other hand, was not as confident. The baby wasn't coming as it should.

They talked about the possibility of a c-section, but Marisol wanted to save that option as a last resort. She had always dreamt of natural childbirth. She was ready to fight for her baby, no matter what it took. The nurses tried to make her as comfortable as possible, but it was her mother's coaching and Hector's cheerleading that made her feel everything was going to be okay.

* * *

Tynise was feeling too ugly and bloated to go anywhere, so she decided to just lie around in her oversized house dress and eat. She munched and crunched handfuls of chips and snack cakes, a junk food junkie descended from a long line of junk food junkies.

The one thing her mother believed in was a full cupboard. She knew she wouldn't be able to give them much in life. There would be no big screen TV or Xbox or rooms full of fancy dolls in matching outfits. But she made sure they never went to bed hungry. There was never a shortage of snacking material in the house. As the oldest, Tynise knew all the good places to hide the best snacks from Quincy and Jasmine.

Tynise found that perfectly comfortable, body molding spot on the sofa and let her mind go numb through a myriad of daytime talk shows, soap operas, game shows, and reality court TV. She spent the day nodding off and on, getting up only to replenish her supply of snacks. The only thing that kept her from a good, deep sleep was a series of strong cramps. She had experienced a lot of cramping over the past few weeks so she didn't think too much about it. The doctor had told her that the little mini contractions were just her uterus getting in shape for delivery and she may even experience false labor before the real thing hit. She simply readjusted her pillows and sunk deeper into the sofa hoping the cramping would subside, but it didn't. All of a sudden a spasm struck that contracted her muscles so hard it felt like a 7.0 earthquake rumbled inside her. She knew it was time, but she didn't panic. The plan was to call her mom at work. Tynise had asked a lot of questions throughout her pregnancy and she had done her homework. She knew that she still had plenty of time between the first labor pains and delivery.

"Tynise, baby, where are you?" Tynise's mother crashed through the door about twenty minutes after she called. "I'm so sorry. I got here as fast as I could."

"Relax, Mom, I'm fine. I've been timin' the contractions and they're still pretty far apart. I've got my bag ready and I left a note for Jasmine and Quincy. I just hope Quincy comes home."

"He will, baby, we talked about it. I've been praying for him,

Tynise. He knows his family needs him now. I don't think he'll let us down. We haven't lost him yet."

"I hope you're right, Mom. Let's just go."

"Sweet Jesus, please don't let the traffic be too bad," Tynise's mother prayed as they hurried to the car. It took about thirty minutes to get to the hospital. By the time they arrived Tynise's contractions had already begun to grow stronger and closer together.

"Ugh, they gettin' worse," Tynise growled as she stepped out of the car gripping her abdomen. "Why they comin' so fast?"

"It's okay, honey, we're here," Tynise's mother replied trying to disguise her trepidation behind a calm voice. "He's just anxious to see you. Don't worry, honey. Try to relax. Women have been birthin' babies since the sweet Lord planted the seed in Eve. It's what we was meant to do. Your body knows what to do naturally. We need to get you inside."

All of a sudden, Tynise felt a unique pressure pushing down on her lower abdomen and a strange liquid gushed down and splattered all over the walkway. But this was more than just water breaking. She had totally lost control of her bodily functions and went number one and number two all at once. The smell was awful.

"Ew, mommy, look," a little girl screamed pointing to Tynise, "it stinks."

"Oh my God. Oh, God," Tynise yelled too embarrassed to lift her head.

"It's okay, baby. That's just your water breaking," her mother reassured. You're okay. Let's get you inside. You're going to be in a comfortable bed soon."

Everyone stared at Tynise and held their noses as she struggled her way through the lobby with a stinky mixture of birth water, poo and pee sliding down her legs. One look at Tynise and the nurses scurried about like ants in a rainstorm as they rushed her to the delivery room.

* * *

159

In a delivery room two doors down Marisol was in her tenth hour of labor writhing in agony over especially strong contractions. The epidural they gave her took the edge off the crippling pain and gave her the strength to persevere, but she found true strength in Hector and her mother. They held her hands, prayed with her and supported her in any way they could. It was hard to watch the person they loved the most go through hell, but there really wasn't much they could do. Marisol alone bore the burden of bearing down and enduring the pain of muscles contorting and bones expanding. She never gave up or even once pleaded to quit. She simply pushed on with the commitment of a climber scaling Mount Everest. Everyone in the room was impressed with her resilience. She was the bravest and most determined expectant mother the hospital staff had ever seen. All were astonished at how courageous a fifteen year old girl could be.

"Miss Mendez, I think its time we prepare you for a c-section," the doctor suggested. "The baby is under stress and you are still not dilated enough for the baby to pass."

"He's right, mi hija," Marisol's mother said as she looked into her weary eyes. "You been working so hard. It's okay. You need to rest now. It's gonna be better for the baby."

"I don't want to give up, Mama. I can do it. I don't want to have no scar," she pleaded as she glanced at Hector.

"I know you can do it," Hector said as he stroked her hair, "but the baby. She needs to come out now. That's all that matters, okay."

Marisol turned her head to hide her eyes and silently nodded. They slipped an I.V. into her arm and she faded into sleep.

* * *

Tynise's baby was ready to greet the world.

"Okay, just breathe deep, in and out, and get ready for one final push," the doctor said as he positioned himself to receive the baby. "The breathing will help with the pain."

"No, it don't," Tynise barked at him, sweating and puffing in and out, "ugh....."

"Come on, Tynise, you're doing great," her mother cheered her on. "I can see the baby's head. Oh, Tynise, it's coming, keep pushing, keep pushing."

"That's right, one more good push just like that," the doctor encouraged. "I've got the head. Give me one more good push and it will all be over soon."

"Ugh.....," Tynise bore down with all her might. There was tearing and stretching and pressure that left her paralyzed with nothing left to do but scream.

For what seemed like forever, the only sound in the room was Tynise's curdling shrieks. Then, she heaved a long sigh, the room was silent for a moment, and her shrieks of pain were replaced by the healthy cries of a beautiful baby boy.

"Oh, sweet Jesus," Tynise's mother exclaimed, throwing her hands to the sky. "Thank you, Jesus. Thank you, Jesus."

Tynise felt an overwhelming sensation of relief. It was finally over. They quickly wiped the baby's eyes and placed him, still covered with afterbirth, on Tynise's chest.

All the nurses congratulated her on a quick delivery. They told horror stories of twenty hour labors and said she should feel lucky that she was only in labor for three hours. But to Tynise, it was the longest three hours of her life.

"What's wrong with his skin?" she asked, frowning at his chafed, wrinkled face covered in gooey slime. She thought he looked more like some kind of alien than a little baby.

"Nothing, honey, they all look like that when they come out. They just need to clean him up. Tynise, I'm so proud of you. What a beautiful baby you made. He looks just like his grandma." Tynise's mother beamed a bright smile at her baby and her baby's baby.

"You think so?" Tynise replied and squintined her eyes at the baby. "I don't see it. Are you sure he's supposed to look like that? I mean, is he okay?"

"He's fine, don't worry. You made a miracle today, Tynise. God has truly blessed us. Thank you, Jesus."

Tynise didn't look up when the nurses took the baby from her arms and turned their backs toward the cleaning station. They cleaned the baby, wrapped him tightly in a blanket and handed him back to Tynise. He was squirming and crying and still so wrinkled Tynise had a hard time recognizing him as her own.

* * *

Marisol woke up to a room full of family. Hector's mother bought back her little brothers who were much better behaved after a good, long nap and a nice plate of tacos for lunch. Her sister and cousin had returned, too. Everyone was there to welcome the new baby into the family.

"Hector," Marisol slowly opened her eyes and called out in a soft, raspy voice. "Hector, where's my baby? Que paso?"

"I'm right here," Hector quickly replied, reading the worry on her face. "It's all good, baby. You did great. We have a beautiful baby girl. You did it."

"Where is she? I want to see her. Where is she? Is she okay? She don't have nothing wrong with her, does she? I want to see her."

"She's perfect, mi hija," her mother said as the rest of the family approached the bed. "They're bringing her in right now. We was just waiting for you to wake up."

As if on cue, a nurse came into the room and placed the baby in Marisol's arms. "You know you gave us all a good scare there for a minute, young lady, but you pulled through like a real trooper," the nurse said smiling at Marisol.

A hush fell upon the room as mother and child instinctively locked eyes. Big and brown with a slight hint of blue in the part that was supposed to be white; the baby's wide open eyes reminded Marisol of pictures she had seen of tranquil Caribbean seas.

"That's right, mi hija, you know your mama, don't you." She gently kissed her baby on the forehead.

Chapter 26

Marisol and Tynise both stayed in the hospital that night Tynise's mom had gone home because she had to be at work early in the morning. Besides, she wouldn't admit it, but she was nervous about leaving Jasmine under Quincy's care for too long. That left Tynise alone with nothing to keep her company but anxiety, doubts, questions and insecurities that kept her tossing and turning all night. She couldn't stop thinking of her son who was sleeping down the hall in the nursery where they kept all the newborns and how much he was going to change her life. She finally decided to go see him.

"Hector," Marisol barked. "Hector, wake up."

"Hey, baby, what's up? Is everything okay?" Hector popped up from the bed the hospital provided for a family member to stay with new mothers.

"I can't sleep. I want to see our baby."

"Okay, we should check on her, right? That's a good idea. What time is it?"

"It's almost five."

"Damn, the sun ain't even up yet, but I guess we're gonna have to get used to that. She's gonna be waking us up in the middle of the night to feed, huh?"

"Si, claro. They say it's gonna be really bad when her teeth come in."

"Are you sure we're ready for all this?"

"We're ready, baby. Everything's gonna be perfect. The baby's room is ready and our parents are gonna help us so much. Come on, help me up."

They eased their way down the hall at a snail's pace. The pain medication was doing its job, but Marisol could still feel the stitches and she didn't want to take any chances. The hallway was quiet except for a nurse shuffling through her paperwork. The nursery was empty except for a solitary, dark, shadowy figure staring through the glass. Hector and Marisol didn't pay it much attention at first, but the figure became more familiar as they approached.

"Dios mi, Tynise," Marisol called out.

"Mari, is that you?" Tynise walked as fast as she could toward Marisol and gave her a hug. They looked at each others stomachs. "You had your baby. Is she okay," Tynise asked.

"She's beautiful, and you?"

"I have a son. Let me show you. He's the one in the back, see?"

"Oh, yes, I see. He's beautiful, Ty."

"Where's yours?"

"My little angel is right here." Marisol pointed. "You see her. We named her Maribel. It means beautiful. "

"That's a really pretty name. It definitely fits. She sure has a lot of hair."

"I know, it's crazy, huh." Hector beamed with pride.

"She is beautiful, Mari. Man, she looks just like you, and you, too, Hector. I can see both of you in her."

"Did you have a hard time?" Marisol asked.

"Well, the nurses didn't seem to think so. But man, that junk hurt like hell. I guess it could have been worse."

"I had to have a c-section."

"Ew, did it hurt?"

"It wasn't so bad, but I'm gonna have a big scar. The doctor said it's gonna look a lot different when it heals, but I don't know. So, what did you name your baby?"

"I haven't come up with a good one yet. You got any

164

suggestions?"

"Hector is a good strong name," Hector said sticking out his chest."

"Right," Tynise said rolling her eyes. "I'll have to think about that one. I ain't thought about it much. I've been to busy thinkin' about how I'm gonna raise him. You guys are so lucky. You have it all figured out. You already have a room for your baby and everything. Mine's gonna have to sleep in the room with me and Jasmine. Anyway, I'm takin' him home later on today."

"They won't let me go for three more days. They got to make sure everything's okay with my stitches and everything, but I can't wait to get Maribel home. So, what time was he born?"

"My water broke around two. Mari, it was awful. It came out all over the sidewalk. I lost it all, if you know what I mean. I had to walk into the hospital with that stinky, junk drippin' all down my legs. Man, that mess was embarrassin'."

"Tynise, that sounds horrible," Marisol gasped and held her hand over her face.

"I had a lot of pain after that. My contractions were really hard from the start, but they keep tellin' me he came pretty fast. I finally pushed him out at five thirty."

"It only took three hours. Aye, you so lucky. I had to go for ten hours before they took her with the c-section. They were worried she wouldn't make it," Marisol said squeezing Hector's hand. "I don't know when the surgery was over."

"The surgery was over around six," Hector interrupted. "The doctor told me her official birth time was ten minutes after six."

"Yes, I had mine first," Tynise smiled secretively at Marisol.

"What are you smiling about," Hector asked, sensing he was being left out on something.

"It's nothing, baby," Marisol giggled at Hector. "She just want her baby to be older than mine."

Tynise, Marisol and Hector sat in the nursery and stared through the window at their babies for a couple more hours. When Marisol and Hector looked at Maribel they could see the future in her eyes.

165

Mark Miller

When Tynise looked at her baby, all she could see was her future slipping away.

Chapter 27

Marisol looked down at her scarred, still slightly swollen belly as she carefully changed a soiled diaper. She discovered a sense of purpose as she ran her fingers across the transformed skin. She didn't think of it as a scar, but a reminder of the pain and struggle she endured, a reminder of her responsibility to care for the beautiful life she created. Then she turned her eyes toward Hector, still stretched out in the bed sound asleep, and she felt the security of not having to bear the responsibility alone. It was everything she had always dreamed of. This was the happiest time of her life.

The quiet of a peaceful house allowed her thoughts to wander. Her happiness turned to remorse when she thought about the babies her friends had lost. She tried to imagine what Ruby's baby would have looked like and wondered if it would have been as beautiful as Maribel. She tried to call Ruby, but there was no answer, just like the other hundred times she had tried to call over the past few days.

"Tynise." Marisol had to share her anxiety with someone else.

"Hey, Mari," a half groggy Tynise answered the phone. "Don't tell me, you're baby's keepin' you up, too?"

"No, Maribel's sleeping okay. How's your baby?"

"He's okay, I guess, but he's been cryin' a lot. Mom said it ain't nothin' to worry about, but I don't know. Does yours cry a lot?"

"No, she don't cry too much. She's just been sleeping. Tynise, I'm worried about Ruby. It's gotta be hard to lose a baby like that. I think we should go see her."

"I know. I ain't heard nothin' from her since we saw her in the hospital."

"We have to go see her. I can get Hector to drive us."

"I want to, but my mom is at work and the baby is too young to be takin' no car ride all the way out there to where Ruby stays. Plus, I gotta watch Jasmine."

"Okay, but me and Hector still gonna go."

"That's cool. I wish I had a mother-in-law to watch my baby whenever I want. Go on without me. Let me know what's up."

Marisol and Hector braced themselves for bad news on the way to Ruby's house. They thought about what it would feel like to have to live with the man who killed your baby and imagined every terrible outcome. Marisol reminded Hector of the fate of one of her favorite novela actresses. Her father was an escaped convict. He returned to his house to find his estranged daughter there alone and decided to lock her up in the bathroom for fear that she might turn him in. By the time they arrived at Ruby's house she had almost convinced Hector that they would find Ruby locked up in some kind of dungeon in the basement.

The first thing they noticed was the run down condition of the usually perfectly manicured yard. Marisol hurried Hector up the winding steps that led to the front door.

"There's no answer," Marisol sighed after ringing the doorbell several times.

"I don't think anybody's home," Hector shouted from in front of the living room window. "I don't see any cars in the garage. Nope, there's nobody home."

"Can I help you?" A white haired, old lady with a squeaky, ankle biting dog hurried up the walkway. "Excuse me. Can I help you?"

"We was looking for my friend," Marisol answered. "Her name is Ruby. Do you know her? She lives in this house."

"I know her." The lady looked at them suspiciously. "Who did you say you were?"

"We're friends of Ruby. She goes to our school," Hector stepped in. "Look, lady, if we were trying to break into the house, do you think I'd be peeking my head through the window in the middle of the day?"

"Please, Ruby's my friend," Marisol pleaded. "She didn't come to school and she don't have no answer on her phone. It just rings. Do you know what happen to her?"

"She is you're friend isn't she?" The lady sensed the anxiety and sincerity in Marisol's voice. "I'm sorry. There's so much crime around these days. You just can't trust people any more. But you look like nice kids, I guess. So, you go to school with Ruby. She is a beautiful young lady, just like her mother. Oh, they look just like a pair of China dolls."

"Yes, ma'am, we go to school with Ruby," Hector interrupted in an impatient tone. "Do you know what happened to her?"

"Well, I assume they've moved," she replied in a tone that let Hector know she was offended by his lack of tact. "I guess it's been about two months now. They packed all their stuff in the SUV one night and took off. Then, they came back a couple of days later with one of those small U-haul trucks. I guess they could've been going on vacation. They did pack up a lot of their stuff, but they left a lot of it behind, too. It would be a shame to think they left all that absolutely gorgeous furniture unattended. Do you think they're coming back?"

"I don't know," Marisol answered solemnly. "I don't know where she is."

169

Mark Miller

Chapter 28

"Tynise," a familiar voice called out to Tynise as she stood in line at the corner store.

"Hey, Mari, what's up?" Tynise turned around and made silly faces at her baby, trying to elicit a smile. "Hey, Maribel, hey beautiful, hey there. Mari, she is such a pretty baby. Look at you. You got you're baby lookin' all cute in that little, pink outfit. Looks like you got this mother thing all worked out."

"Thank you, Tynise. I'm sorry I didn't have time to call you more since we left the hospital. Maribel got me so busy. So, where's your baby? What did you name him?"

"I didn't." Tynise paused and looked down at her feet trying to hide her eyes. "I gave him up for adoption, Mari. I just couldn't do it. It was so crowded in my room. I couldn't stand it. And he was so hard to take care of. I mean, he never stopped crying."

"I know it can be hard, Tynise, but you just gave him away?"

"Please don't look at me like that. It was so hard. I didn't think I would be able to do it at first, but my mom hooked me up with this really great adoption place. I even got to pick out the parents myself."

Tynise read the disappointment Marisol's face. "Look, Mari, I knew I wouldn't be able to raise him right, so I hand picked a couple that could do right by him. It's like I got to plan his future, even if I

170

ain't gonna be around to see it. Anyway, he lives with a nice, rich, lawyer and his wife in San Francisco. I got to meet them and they really cool people. They gonna be great parents to him. Mari, he's gonna have everything I could never give him. Think about it. He's gonna go to a good school, in a good neighborhood. You should see that house. Trust me, they livin' large. You ain't gonna find no gangs or crack heads runnin' up and down the streets where he lives. If he stayed here, he would've just ended up like Darnell or Quincy, runnin' the streets or in jail. I thought it through with my mom. I know I did the right thing by him. My baby is gonna have a good life. Even if I couldn't give him nothin' else, I gave him that. Isn't that the most important thing?"

"I guess so. I don't know. Are you happy? Can you live with it?"

"I think so. I guess I don't have a choice now, do I?"

"I think you can, Tynise. I think you did the best thing for you. If you happy with it, I'm gonna be happy for you."

"Whaaaaa," Maribel let out a loud wail.

"Que paso, mi hija, tienes hambre?" Marisol smiled at her baby. "I gotta go, Tynise. When she get hungry, she gotta eat. I'm not gonna do it in front of all the people. I did it before in the park, but I didn't have no choice. I just whip it out and feed her in front of everybody. Aye, it was crazy."

"Whaaaaa."

"Okay, mi hija, we gonna go. Tynise, you gotta come by the house. How come you don't hang out on the porch no more?" Marisol asked as she leaned into Tynise for a goodbye hug.

"I don't know. It just didn't seem right without Lauryn and Ruby there, you know. Anyway, I didn't think you guys were hanging out any more now that you're in the family way."

"That is the family way. We live at Hector's but you know everybody still be hanging out on Mama's porch."

"Okay, I'll come by. I have to pick up my prize, anyway." Tynise smiled."

"Prize?"

171

"Oh, don't act like you don't know what I'm talkin' about. You know I won the bet. I may not have my baby with me, but he was born first."

"Si, claro. I forget. So, did you know what you want yet?"

"I don't know. Maybe one of those bracelets you got, the ones with the fancy Mexican designs or the ear rings. I don't know yet."

"Whaaaaa."

"Okay, mi hija. We gonna go right now. Whatever you want to pick, Tynise. I'll see you later, okay."

Tynise felt good as Marisol smiled and rushed away with her crying baby. She felt happy for Marisol, knowing that she had the baby she wanted with the boyfriend she loved. But she felt better for herself and the decision she had made. There would be plenty of time for crying babies after she finished college.

Looking around the hood on her way home, Tynise saw enough evidence to convince herself she made the right decision. *At least he ain't gonna be dealin' with these, bums always begging. He's gonna be shopping at one of those nice, clean mega malls where they call the police on beggers. When he opens his eyes, he won't see no trash, no broken glass, no graffiti all over nasty, broken down buildings. He'll be around them pretty yards and parks with grass where the kids run and play. He'll fall sleep listening to crickets and wake up to bird songs. When he fights, it's gonna be with some punk, white boy, not some gang banger trying to get him into drugs and stuff. Damn, I wish I could go with him.*

She always felt a twinge of despair when she approached the project where she lived, but today she felt solace knowing her son would never have to call such a place home. It gave her the hope to believe and dream for herself. If her son could make it out, maybe, with the money she got from the adoption, she could make it out, too.

"Tynise."

She jerked around to find the voice, but didn't see anyone but the same old guys that hang out all day, everyday.

"Tynise, what's up?"

This time the voice was more familiar, but it couldn't be, could it? She jerked her head again to follow the voice.

"Don't act like you don't know me, now."

"Lauryn, is that you," Tynise had to do a double take to recognize her best friend. *This skinny, little, tore up skank walkin' toward me can't be my Lauryn. What's up with that raggedy skirt all dirty and tore up? What happened to her hair? Lauryn be actin' crazy sometimes, but she always looked tight. She ain't never come out with her hair looking like that, all jacked up and greasy.*

"What's up, Ty? Long time, no see," Lauryn said as she gave Tynise a hug.

Tynise was overwhelmed by the dark, grey circles around her eyes that made her look twenty years older and she could no longer hold back. "What the hell happened to you, Lauryn?"

"What? Oh, you mean this skirt. I just ain't had no time to wash clothes, that's all," Lauryn answered while she tugged at her clothes and stroked her hair.

"Why are your hands shakin'? What you been doin'?"

"I ain't been doin' nothin'. I've been clean, Ty, for real. I gotta be. Ty, I'm pregnant again. I'm gonna be a mother just like you. I may be comin' in late, but I'm still in the Baby Club."

"What! Lauryn, are you crazy? Look at you. You ain't ready to be nobody's mother. God, man, what are you on?"

"I ain't on nothin'. I told you."

"Then stop shakin'. If you ain't on nothin', stop shakin'."

"Stop it, Tynise. Why you trippin'? You're a mother. You should be happy for me. I'm happy for you. How's your baby. Damn, it's been so long since I seen you. Did you have a boy or a girl?"

"I had a boy, Lauryn, but he ain't with me no more."

"What? What happened?"

"I gave him up for adoption. It was the best thing, believe me."

"No way, Tynise. How could you?"

"How could I not? Lauryn, my son is gonna grow up in a nice neighborhood in San Francisco. What did I have to give him here?

173

What do you have to give your baby? Can you even raise a baby? What you doin' for money? You still sellin' your body down at that club? Is that the life you want for your baby? Think about it, Lauryn. This ain't no joke. It's a human life and you the one responsible for it."

"I know, Tynise. I'm straight, for real. Man, first Ruby lost her baby then you gave yours away. What about Mari? Tell me she didn't lose hers, too."

"No, she didn't. Mari has a beautiful baby girl named Maribel. She and Hector stay together with the baby over at Hector's house. I just saw her right now at the store. She looks good and her baby is beautiful."

"See, Mari did it. If she could do it, I can do it, too."

"Yeah, but Mari's in a totally different situation. First of all, she has her man right by her side to help her. They stay in a nice house and they got a room to themselves and for the baby. Plus, Hector's mother is always at home to watch the baby, so they can both go back to school. And Mari's mother takes care of the baby all the time, too. She said they spend more time at her mama's house, you know, just hanging on the porch, than they do at Hector's house."

"Sounds like she got the hook up, for real. I'm happy for her. Hey, I gotta go see somebody." Lauryn abruptly shifted her attention when she spotted a short, young man standing alone on the corner across the street. "Man, I can't believe that junk about your baby. That's a trip, but I wanna see Mari's baby, for real. I'm a come see it, for real. Tell Mari and Hector I said what's up," Lauryn yelled and ran across the street.

"Lauryn, wait," Tynise called out, but she knew Lauryn wasn't going to turn around. She recognized the young man across the street as one of the biggest dealers on the block.

Chapter 29

"Mari, Mari, come get the phone," Hector's mother shouted down the hallway.

"Who is it?"

"I don't know. She said she's a friend of yours."

"Hello," Marisol answered the phone apprehensively.

"Hey, Mari, it's me, Ruby."

"Ruby! Dios mio, Ruby. What happened? Where are you?"

"I'm okay. I'm staying with my mother at her sister's in New York."

"New York City?"

"Yeah, Queens, Mari, it's a trip. There're so many different kinds of people here, all mixed up, living together."

"What about your father? Did the police get him?"

"No, they didn't. It was like I thought. He got this high powered lawyer and the army totally backed him up. You should have seen that lying lawyer at work. By the time he was done, he had the jury believing my father was some kind of great, war hero or something. It was his word against ours and we really couldn't prove anything."

"So, he just gonna get away with it."

"Yeah, I guess so. But, you know, Mari, it didn't turn out all bad."

"What do you mean?"

"Well, my mother, she turned out to be okay after all. She had my back through the whole thing. She told me my father had been beating on her for years. She just took it because she didn't want to break up our family. I found out family means more to her than I thought. But she said she never thought he would turn on me. When he did, that was the last straw."

"Aye, Ruby, que horrible."

"I know. I was too caught up doing my own thing to notice how he treated her. Now I know why she always drank so much. But everything's going to be okay now. He's not going to jail, but she fixed it so he can't ever bother us again. If he does he's gonna get kicked out of the army and lose his pension. She's gonna divorce him and the judge said since I'll be turning eighteen in three years I could make my own decision whether or not I want to see him. And I definitely don't want to see him ever again."

"That's good, Ruby. I'm so happy for you and your mother."

"I know. We're closer now than we've ever been before. It was amazing to find out how much we had in common when we started talking to each other. I was always jealous of the way you could talk with your mother. Now I know what I was missing. I don't know why we never talked before."

"So, are you going to stay in New York?"

"I don't know, but I think we're gonna be here for a while. My aunt's place isn't as nice as the old house, but it's nice. Mom said she's selling the old house. Too many memories there, you know. She really wants to make a clean break. She said he wasn't gonna contest the divorce, as long as his precious military career isn't tarnished. After everything he put her through over the years, he's gonna have to pay a grip in alimony. I bet we can get enough money from selling the house to buy a smaller place, maybe around here, and make sure I can go to any college I want."

"That's great, Ruby. I'm so happy for you."

"Listen to me going on and on. What's up with you? Did you have your baby okay?"

"Oh, yes, I have a beautiful girl. We named her Maribel."

"Oh, thank God. I was almost afraid to ask after what happened to me and Lauryn. What about Tynise?"

"You not gonna believe it. Me and Tynise had our babies at the same time over at St Joseph's."

"No way. Were you in the same delivery room?"

"No. I had labor for, like, ten hours and I had a c-section, but she just pop her baby out. She only had labor for three hours."

"Really, what did she have?"

"She had a boy."

"Man, a boy and a girl. I can't wait to see them both."

"I can't wait for you to meet Maribel. I know she gonna love you. But, Tynise, she don't have her son no more. She gave him up to adoption."

"Are you kidding me? Why did she do that? I thought she really wanted her baby."

"So did I. I don't know. I think her mother talk her out of it. But she talk like she don't want the baby, too. She keep talking about how much money you need for a baby and that it's gonna be too hard to raise him."

"Well, you know Tynise's family doesn't have a lot of money. I mean, it would have been very hard for her."

"It's not so hard. I don't have no money, but my baby is okay."

"Yeah, Mari, but you have a lot of support between Hector, his parents and your parents. Tynise only has her mother and she's busting her butt as it is just to keep above water. I don't know if I could have given my baby up for adoption, but I can see why she made that decision. I've had a lot of time to think about it and you really need to be straight before you think about having a baby. It would have been really hard for her to raise her baby on her own."

"But she wasn't gonna be alone. We was gonna help her."

"I know, Mari. I'm not saying I could do it. I'm just saying I know what it feels like to feel like you're all alone, even when people are trying to help you. I don't know. Sometimes things just turn out for the best. Don't get me wrong. I'm always gonna miss my baby, but things would have been all messed up if I had it. I would

Mark Miller

have been fighting with my mother all the time. I don't know. They say everything happens for a reason. Maybe it just wasn't my time."

"I don't know either, Ruby. I just leave it up to God and I pray for my family and my friends. I'm gonna pray for you and Tynise and Lauryn. Tynise said she's still doing the drugs."

"I can't say I'm surprised to hear that. That girl is crazy."

"Aye, Ruby, I gotta go. Maribel is crying. Promise me you'll come and see her. She got to get to know her Aunt Ruby."

"Okay, Mari, I will. I promise I'll stay in touch."

"Okay, I gotta go. I'll talk to you later. Bye, Ruby."

"Bye, Mari."

Marisol scolded her self for not getting Ruby's phone number before she hung up, but she soon forgot all about it as she rushed to answer Maribel's escalating cries.

"Baby, where you been," Hector said, bouncing the baby up in down in his arms with a frustrated look on his face. "She don't want to stop crying."

"Let me have her." Marisol took the baby, held her close to her heart, and began rocking back and forth. "Shhh, shhh, mi hija, it's okay, mama's here, shhh."

"Damn, how come I can't do that?" Hector chuckled as he watched Marisol lull his daughter back to sleep. "How did you learn how to be such a good mother so quick?"

"I don't know. Watching my mama, I guess. Now be quiet. She's falling asleep again."

"So, who was that on the phone?" Hector asked in a whisper.

"Oh, you're not gonna believe it. It was Ruby."

"Really, what's up with your girl?"

"She moved with her mother to stay with her aunt in New York. She said her mother's getting a divorce."

"That's good. She better leave that bastard after what he did."

"I know. I was so happy for her. I think she's gonna be okay."

"Is Maribel asleep?" Hector said in a soft voice.

"Yes, I think so."

"Then come here. I want to tell you something."

Hector gently pulled on Marisol's arm and guided her to sit next to him on the bed. He was quiet and had a serious look on his face that made Marisol nervous.

"What's wrong?" she asked.

"Nothing, baby, it's just that," he hesitated to catch his breath, "man, this is hard. Look, I have something for you. Close your eyes."

"Hector, stop playing."

"Come on, just do it, please."

Hector reached into his top dresser drawer and pulled something out from underneath a pile of freshly folded t-shirts. "Now hold out your hands." He knelt down on one knee in front of her and said, "You know I love you, baby. I didn't even realize how much until you gave me Maribel. You're so good with her. We're all so good together. Open your eyes, baby."

"Hector, Dios mio, Hector," Marisol gasped as she looked at the modest diamond ring lying in her open hand.

"Mari, will you marry me?"

The words rang through her ears like the sweet melody of the first song birds of spring and tears ran down her face. "Si, Hector, claro. I will marry you."

They stood up, held each other tightly and rocked silently back and forth to the rhythm of their heart beats.

"I'm gonna do right by you and our family, baby. I promise you that."

"I know you will, Hector. We gonna have a beautiful life together. You gonna be a great father. I'm so happy Maribel gonna grow up in he same house where her papi grow up."

"What do you mean? She ain't gonna grow up around here, not all her life anyway. Baby, I'm planning on something better for our children. I want to be able to move out of here in four to five years, when I graduate from college and get a good job. Don't you want to raise our children in a neighborhood where they don't have to deal with crack heads and gang bangers?"

179

"I don't know. I like living here, con la familia. And I want Maribel to know her grandparents."

"I know, but we can always come back to visit. It's not like we're gonna move far away, but we have to think about what's best for our family now. We could get one of those townhouses they got over in Oak Park. It's so clean over there, you know, and they say the schools are the best."

"Look at you, all responsible and everything."

"I have to be, you know. I got to take care of my girls." They both turned to smile at Maribel.

"Don't get me wrong. I ain't never gonna forget where I came from, for real. In a way, I'm glad I came up in the hood. I learned a lot about life from the streets. You can't be no punk around here, you know. But I don't want my kids coming up in this mess. You know I ain't gonna have Maribel dealing with all these little busters around here. We got to give her better."

"I know. I can't believe I found you," Marisol said, looking at Hector with admiration. She always loved it when he talked about his plans for the future. He was the only boy she ever met that talked about anything other than money, drugs, sports, or sex.

"Why do you think I always worked so hard in school? At least we have an opportunity here. All I have to do is work hard and have a plan and I can get mine. I'm gonna get that American dream. You better believe that. Remember how hard our parents had it in Mexico."

"I know. I hate it when they tell the stories of how poor everything is there. I'm so glad we moved here when I was a little girl."

"That's right," Hector continued. He was on a roll. "We could have grown up like our parents, in Mexico where the best job we could get only pays a few dollars a day. I know I'm lucky to be here. At least I have the opportunity to get over. The hood inspired me to do better."

"Inspired you?"

"Yeah, coming up in the hood inspires you to want to work hard so you can get out of here and make a better life for yourself and your family. It all depends on how you look at it. For me, the hood is the land of inspiration."

Marisol smiled and said, "Tynise and Lauryn would be laughing if they could hear you now. You know you just come up with another name for the hood."

"Yeah, what's that?"

"The *Land of Inspiration.*"

Mark Miller

Also by Mark Miller:

The Inner Light

Out of every dark corner a light will shine. Trouble is born into a life of drugs and gangs, a world of darkness. When his mother is arrested, he discovers a unique gift. He sees an inner light that emanates from the faces of people who treat him well. Follow Trouble as the light guides him through the foster care and juvenile justice systems, the void of an absent mother, and a quest to find his inner light.

Chasing Faith

Cara was always a good Catholic school girl, but when her mother dies from an unexpected drug overdose she begins to question her way of life. Join this intelligent, courageous, young woman as she attempts to find a way to overcome the death of her mother, find a relationship with her estranged father, find her place in the world, and find a way to believe in God.

To information regarding *Baby Club*, *The Inner Light*, or *Chasing Faith*, visit:

www.markmilleronline.net

www.ingramcontent.com/pod-product-compliance
Lightning Source LLC
Chambersburg PA
CBHW050941120626
46552CB00001B/315